IMPERFECTLY CRIMINAL

MARY FRAME

Cover design by Najla Qamber Designs
Editing by Haestella.
Any errors contained herein are likely the result of the author continuing to change/edit after the line edits were completed.

For my mom, Elizabeth Baines.
The strongest woman I know.

1

Love all men. Except lawyers.

—Irish Proverb

**reya**

It’s unmistakable, the sound a body makes when it connects with the front of your car.

I yelp and slam on the brakes just in time to see legs flailing in the air before disappearing to the ground, the view of the body blocked by the rounded hood of my old VW Beetle.

Dear mother of God.

I just ran someone over.

Slamming the stick shift into park, I fumble with the seatbelt, race out of my vehicle and stop dead in my tracks when I see a familiar blond head on the ground.

Holy mother of all shitballs.

I didn't just run over some random pedestrian. I ran over the biggest, baddest, most unfeeling person I've ever met who happens to find me the stupidest and most irritating person *he's* ever met.

He's unconscious. There are books and papers all around him and his bag is lying busted open, about two feet away from the body.

The body.

It's not my fault. There's been construction in front of my apartment building all week, blocking the sidewalk and forcing pedestrians into the street. There are giant trucks and machines all over the place, making it impossible to see what's coming from beyond.

I fall to my knees, laying my head on his chest. He's still breathing. I'm not sure that's a good thing. Once he regains consciousness, he's going to kill me.

I remove my head from his chest and pat him gently on the cheek.

"Mob guy," I say. Dang it, I can never remember his name!

Nothing.

I smack him a little harder. "Mob guy!"

His eyelid twitches slightly.

I'm about to punch him in the face when his eyes blink open. He looks dazed for a second, but then those intense, laser-blue eyes focus right on me.

"You," he says.

"Yeah. It's me," I confirm.

Six months earlier...

"I'm looking for the mob guy!" I yell into the ear of the dude guarding the entrance to the warehouse-turned-boxing-match.

The fight hasn't started yet. There are still a million people in line behind me and I've waited thirty minutes only to be informed I needed to hand over five bucks to even get in to this dump.

The guy doesn't seem to register what I've just said.

"Five dollars!" he yells back, for the second time.

"I don't need to get in, I need to find the guy in charge," I try to explain.

He shakes his bald head. "He never shows up to these things anymore. Now five dollars or get out of here. You're blocking the line."

"Where can I find him?"

This question gets me an utterly incredulous look. "You think I'm going to tell you where he lives?"

"I'll give you the five dollars."

He laughs. "That's not worth my neck. Now move," he says with a jerk of his thumb.

Damn it. I keep hearing about this mob guy, but actually finding him is like nailing down a worm dripping in baby oil. He's like a riddle, wrapped in an enigma, shrouded in mystery, and covered in...something that makes him invisible.

This whole "getting a guy to beat up my evil ex" is harder than I expected.

"Can I at least get a message to him somehow?"

The guy at the door is getting annoyed with me. I know this because he says, "You're really annoying. Go on in and find the ref. His name's Jose. He reports to Dean every night after the fight."

"Dean?"

This gets me another look. "Uh, the guy you're looking for?"

"Right, right." I nod like I knew this.

Mob boss guy has a name. Dean. I'll have to remember that.

I enter the crowded warehouse without having to fork over my five dollars, so I give a big mental "suck my fat one" to the bald dude at the door.

When I first heard about the fights, I didn't think much of it. I've never understood the male compulsion to beat one another into bloody pulps and walk away better friends for it, and watching it is not something I enjoy. But when I heard about the guy who runs these things around the same time my boyfriend the superdouche went to the dark side, I knew. I could hire him to kick Cameron's ass, therefore making Cameron suffer and making me feel...better.

I can't believe how packed the warehouse is. It's a giant space, but it's filled with people, most of whom are crowding around the boxing ring. I have no idea how this is pulled off. There's a new fight every weekend, and every time, there's also a new location. No one knows where it will be until the day of, and then the word spreads through campus like people spreading through Walmart on Black Friday.

I should have brought someone with me—heading into the dark corners of town late at night doesn't seem like the best decision—but I didn't feel like spilling my sob story to anyone after my horrible experience in the peer counseling clinic the other day. I totally lost it. I was a blubbering, sloppy, train wreck of epic proportions. When I mentioned the revenge idea to the chick at the clinic—who looked like she was sixteen and talked like she was sixty—she made me feel like an idiot.

I wander through the crowd, trying to find anyone who looks like they're in charge, but everyone seems to be waiting for the fight to begin. This Jose guy is probably near the ring, I rationalize, heading in that direction. The crowd gets increasingly thicker the closer I get to where the action will be, but finally I make out a group of people that seem to know something. One of them is wearing a black-and-white striped shirt with the words, f*uck with the ref die like the rest* sewed in red lettering on the back, and hot pink, super tight, teeny tiny shorts. Must be Jose.

I stand on the outskirts of their little group for an embarrassingly long time, trying to get someone's attention or make eye contact, but it's not happening. I catch snippets of their conversation.

"How much so far?" the ref asks.

Someone answers, but I can't hear the response.

"You've got to be shitting me!" some chick covered in tattoos and topped with dreadlocks yells.

"What do you mean Johnson's pulling out? He can't do that!"

"Ha...Johnson's pulling out," I snicker. Nobody hears.

"He's going to flip a fucking gasket," the ref says.

Some dude with giant seventies-style sunglasses and a fedora walks up and says something I can't hear over all the talking and noise.

"Did you call him?" Girl with dreads asks.

"Yes I called him, what the fuck else was I gonna do?" Giant glasses says.

"Well, is he coming?"

"He's on his way, he said he's going to fight himself."

"Shut the fuck up."

"Uh, is Dean on his way?" I ask loudly.

Now they hear me. All eyes flick to me.

"Who are you?" dreadlock girl asks.

Shit. What do I tell them? This might be my only chance to talk to this guy.

"I'm his sister."

Dreadlock girl crosses her arms over her chest and eyes me up and down. "His sister?"

"Step sister," I say quickly.

She opens her mouth, but then the crowd gets louder, the roar of voices starts outside and rolls in like a wave. I can't hear anything except the ref guy who's on my immediate right.

"He's here," he says.

And then I'm being pushed around by people clamoring the stage and jolting me this way and that. For a second, I can't breathe and I'm worried I'm going to be swallowed by the horde, but then the ref is yanking me along with him, around the ring and through the madness to a small door just behind the ropes.

It's dark and the space feels enclosed. I freak for a minute, wondering why this guy dragged me in here. What if he's going to hurt me? What if he knows I'm lying and he's going to tie me up, torture the truth out of me, work me over with brass knuckles and those things that pull out people's fingernails until I crack?

I'm a total wuss, I won't last a second. I'm about to yell, "I'm not his sister!" when a light flicks on. I blink against the sudden brightness. The hanging bulb swings to reveal a small room. No windows, just a bench, a small counter with shelves, and another door leading outside which the ref is opening to let in...Thor.

No wait, it's not Thor, but it looks a hell of a lot like him.

If this is torture, sign me up.

"Hey man," ref claps Thor on the back. "Your sister's here, I thought I should keep her safe."

Thor is Mob guy?

He looks shocked and then pissed for a split second before a calm settles over his features. "My sister? Where is she?" he asks, voice hard.

"Here." Ref points in my direction.

Thor's eyes flick to me and he blinks.

"Heyyy...brother!" I say before he can speak. It's like I can't control myself. I know he knows I'm not his sister, but that doesn't stop me from continuing the charade and stepping up and hugging him. Awkwardly. He's got a giant gym bag strapped over his shoulder and I pat it instead of his back.

"Uh, could you give us a sec?" Mob guy says. He hasn't moved. I feel like I'm hugging a giant, immobile boulder.

For a minute, I think he's speaking to me, telling me to leave, so I step back but before I can get very far, I realize the ref's already leaving. The noise from outside fills the small space for a second before the door slams shut and the sound is reduced to a hum.

"Who are you and what do you want?" His voice is flat. He shrugs the bag off his shoulder and sets it on the counter top.

"I have a proposition for you."

He doesn't turn around, just rummages through his things, pulling out boxing gloves and strips of linen. "Look, I'm not into the whole role playing thing and I'm not interested in whatever proposition you have. You can leave out the back door."

I can feel myself flushing, the heat rising up my face.

"It's not that kind of proposition," I say, more firmly than I thought possible after he just implied that I was there to try and sleep with him or *role-play*? As his sister? Has this happened to him before? Gross.

"Then what do you want? I have a thousand people waiting out there. Make it quick." He pulls his shirt over his head, exposing a muscled back and my mouth goes dry.

"I just...I want you to beat up my boyfriend."

Ex-boyfriend, I meant to say, but he's got me all flabbergasted with the skin and the muscle and the...a mini George Takei is *oh my*ing in my head.

He stops rummaging through his stuff and turns to face me. Slowly.

He looks even better from the front than from the behind. Holy hell.

I swallow and remind myself why I'm here, and it's not to hit on some guy, even if he is lickable. "I'll pay you," I add into the silence.

He just stares at me, expression flat. Maybe that girl in the peer counseling clinic was right. This is crazy. What made me think this was a good idea in the first place? Ugh. I'm always doing this, throwing myself into ridiculous situations and getting in way over my head. What's wrong with me?

"Is your boyfriend waiting in the ring right now?" Mob guy asks.

"Um...no."

"Then no." He turns away again. "Have a nice life."

"Please? I'll pay you. A hundred bucks." I sound pathetic, even to my own ears, but I've come too far to turn back now.

My whininess must affect him somewhat.

He drags a frustrated hand through his shaggy blond hair. "Why should I beat up your boyfriend? Why don't you just break up with him?"

"I did break up with Cameron. He's not my boyfriend anymore. He's an asshat and he really deserves to be in some sort of physical pain."

I'm not kidding. He deserves more than pain. He

deserves some kind of curse that makes his willy turn green and fall off.

"So you're the judge and jury, and I'm the executioner?" He begins wrapping a thin band of long fabric around one hand, back still to me.

"Something like that."

He laughs but the sound isn't a happy one. "Listen, uh...?"

"Freya," I supply.

"Yeah. I'm sure your ex-boyfriend Calvin—"

"Cameron."

"Whatever. Wait." He stops and turns, his eyes meeting mine, dark and focused. "Cameron who?"

"Cameron Myers."

"I'll do it."

He answers way too quickly.

"Wait, what?"

"I'll do it," he says a little bit louder. "Pay me fifty bucks now and fifty bucks once it's done. And you'll have your proof by next Thursday."

"That was the quickest one-eighty I've ever witnessed."

He lets out an irritated sigh. "Listen Freddie—"

"Freya," I correct, but he's still talking.

"I don't have time to haggle with you. Take it or leave it."

"I'll take it." I stick my hand out. He eyes it dubiously for a second before giving me a quick, bone-crushing shake with his unwrapped hand.

"Great. Now get the hell out of here. Pay the man at the door." And then his back is to me again.

What a jerk.

"Fine. Pretty sure I met my asshole quotient for the day two minutes into this conversation, and now my cup runneth over," I say as I'm heading for the exit. I'm not sure, but I think I hear him laugh just before the door slams shut behind me.

2

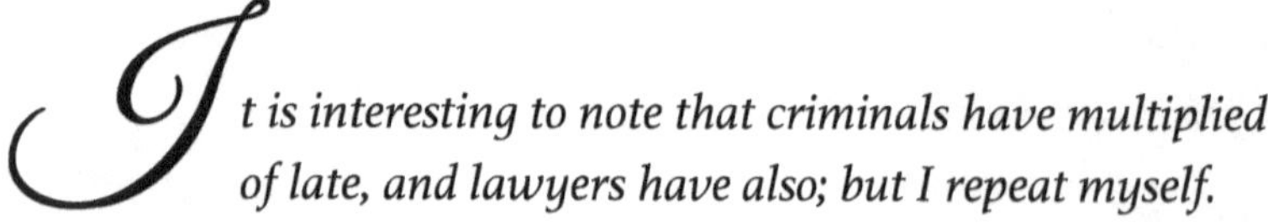

It is interesting to note that criminals have multiplied of late, and lawyers have also; but I repeat myself.

—Mark Twain

Freya

Present day

"Did you hit me with your car?"

"Uh, no?"

Mob guy groans and lifts himself into a sitting position.

I shift away from him, rocks and gravel from the road digging into my knees.

"The evidence suggests otherwise," he grates out, looking over at my still-running vehicle located right in front of us.

"It was an accident."

"You are a walking, talking accident."

"I couldn't see you past the machine thingy." I gesture weakly and stand up, wiping the front of my dress with my hands. The nerve of this man. I swear, every interaction I've had with him ends with me feeling like a jackass and wanting to kick him in the shin. Which might be a bad idea since I just hit him with my car and he was unconscious less than a minute ago. Plus he's roughly the size of a small mountain range.

In order to protect him from further injury at my hands —I can't always control myself—I move back towards my car.

He gets to his feet slowly, shaking out his arms and legs and stretching his neck. "Where do you think you're going?"

"We've made it to that point in our conversation where you're openly mocking me, so I feel like you're gonna survive. Have a nice life."

"You can't just leave."

"I can do what I want."

"No, you can't."

"Yes I can." I open the car door. "I have a date." I don't know why I feel the need to mention that. It's not like he gives a crap. "Besides, you're fine."

Before I can make a move to get in the car and escape, an all too familiar *woop woop* sound fills the air.

I turn in time to see a police car parking directly behind me.

"Shitty bitch snacks," I mutter.

"Or instant karma," Mob guy says.

"Is everything okay over here?" The officer asks, moving towards us. He's fairly young. I would say late twenties, early thirties with a high and tight haircut topping his dark head.

"Everything's fine," I say.

"She hit me with her car."

"Shut up!" The words fly out of my mouth.

"And she's verbally harassing me."

"Did you hit him, ma'am?" The cop is standing on the other side of my door. I'm holding onto the handle like a lifeline.

"It was an accident," I say.

"Have you had anything to drink today?"

I shrug. "Just some water infused with mint and lemon."

"So you'll consent to a breathalyzer?"

I can't do anything but stare into his hard, unblinking eyes. This is not my life.

I sigh and nod. "Yes."

Nearly an hour later, I've been breathalyzed, scolded and ticketed for reckless driving. I've remembered that mob guy's name is actually Dean (well, I didn't really remember, the cop has been saying it since he viewed our IDs).

Both Dean and the officer informed me that I could also be hit with a civil suit if Dean decides to press charges.

The cop offers to call an ambulance to treat Dean's wounds, but he refuses medical treatment.

"Are you going to sue me?" I ask after the cop leaves and Dean's picking up his bag off the ground. I'm standing behind my open car door, like it's a shield from his anger. He hasn't bothered to hide his irritation at me, but that's nothing new.

"Probably." His voice is emotionless and monotone.

"Why?"

"Why not? You drive like an eighty-year-old woman with a lead foot and a lust for blood." He shoves a book into his bag and slings it over his broad shoulder.

"But you're okay," I say.

"Yeah, I'm okay. A few bruised ribs, probably. I've suffered worse. But what about the next poor shmuck? You could kill someone. Maybe this way you'll be more careful."

"Fine." It's pointless arguing with him. "I have to go. You have my info." We exchanged numbers and insurance information somewhere in between walking a straight line and reciting the alphabet backwards, which is really difficult to do, I might add, drunk or not.

I start my car and very carefully check all of my mirrors, making sure Dean is fully out of the way so that I'm not tempted to hit him again, before pulling out and down the road. My date better be spectacular. I need something, anything, to get my mind off the potential law suit breathing down my neck. Like I don't have enough to worry about.

Stopping at a red light, I take a deep breath to calm my

heart and try to get my head straight before I get to the restaurant. There's nothing I can do about the Dean situation right now. I'll just have to wait him out. Let him cool off and try to talk him out of filing charges. Maybe I can get him to drop it if I give him something in return.

A sudden image of both of us naked and sweaty infiltrates my thoughts.

Stupid brain.

He would be attractive if he wasn't such an asshole.

I push him from my mind. I need to concentrate on the problem at hand.

My date.

I hope this time it's different.

Ever since Cameron...ever since we broke up, well, I can't stand to have people touch me. Guys, specifically. It's ridiculous. Even a simple pat on the shoulder makes me jump like I've been shocked, or I run away like a frightened rabbit if they seem too interested in me. I've been dating every male I can find within a twenty-mile radius to get over this problem of mine, and so far, nothing has helped. Maybe tonight is the night. I don't believe it, but hope is the only thing keeping me going at this point.

Cameron left me broken and battered. Not on the outside, but on the inside. Not only did he cheat on me with Liz the slut, he...I can't even think about it. Suffice it to say, he's the reason I can't handle being touched.

I hate that he still has that kind of power over me. Especially since I haven't even talked to the guy in five months.

Luckily, I'm not one of those girls that's easily defeated. I'm not going to let someone else control me. The problem is that no matter how I try, I can't make myself stop having these involuntary reactions.

Since we broke up, I figured it would help me get over him if I could find someone else, someone who is the exact opposite of everything Cameron is and everything he represents (read: pure evil bastard). Once I find this paragon of virtue, I could sleep with him a million times (or so), until Cameron is no more than a distant and vague recollection.

Great idea, right? That is if I can get past the whole part where they actually have to touch me.

I pull up outside the restaurant and check myself in my rearview mirror before getting out of the car. I see my date, Mike, standing outside the door. I know it's him because we agreed he would wear a red tie and a black suit. He's cute, in a clean-cut, Zac-Efron-before-rehab kind of way. He's not very tall, but I don't care about that since I am five foot nothing. It doesn't take much to tower over me. My friend Bethany set us up, and all I know is that he's pre-med and according to Bethany, one of the nicest guys ever.

"Here goes nothing."

3

When a man is denied the right to live the life he believes in, he has no choice but to become an outlaw.

–Nelson Mandela

Dean

I watch Freya drive away. A small triangle of fabric from her dress sticks out of the car door, flapping in the breeze.

I can't help but smile. She's a mess.

And she just hit me with her car.

Why am I smiling?

I frown.

My phone rings before I can think too much about it.

"What's up kiddo?"

"I'm not a kid, I'll be thirteen in November," the immediate response fills my ear.

"A fact that I'm well aware of, no matter how much I try to forget." I kick at a rock in the middle of the sidewalk, sending it skittering into the street.

"What are you doing right now?" Sarah asks.

I scrub a hand through my hair and sigh. I love my little sister, I really do, but it's never a good thing when she calls and asks that question.

"I'm on my way to the library. What do you need?"

There's a momentary pause and then she says, "Mom's sleeping and there's no food in the house."

"What do you mean, there's no food? We just went shopping last week."

Sarah sighs and I can hear her opening and shutting cupboards. I can picture her in the faded kitchen, all gangly limbs and blond hair that's messier than mine. I should have bought more food last week. Lately, Sarah's been eating more than two full-grown men.

"Well, I'm hungry, like, all the time. I can't help it, I'm growing," she grumbles.

"I know you are." I squint down the road in the direction of campus, trying to pull my thoughts together. I had planned on going to the library. There's a guy I need to scope out for a job next week, and he's supposed to be there today.

But now...I could run to the store and come back to campus later. It sort of wrecks the time I would have spent studying, but I'll have time to find my target, at least.

At the rate Sarah eats, I'm going to need even more jobs than I already have.

"All that's left is a can of refried beans and a tub of mayonnaise," she says.

I'm already walking back towards my car. "I'll be there in twenty," I say before we hang up.

I would jog to save time, but my body's still a bit sore from the impact of Freya's car. I'm lucky she wasn't going very fast.

It's probably sadistic, but I almost enjoyed making her feel bad. Making her indebted to me, in some way. Knowing that I'll have to talk to her again. It's weird because she's not exactly my type. Not that I have a type, anymore. I don't have time for romance. I don't have time for much more than working, studying and taking care of my family.

I don't really know why, but I love messing with her. She gets this indignant expression that's almost cute. And the things that come out of her mouth. You really can't predict it.

Once I'm at the car, I throw my bag in the back and slide into the driver's seat.

I always park a good long way from campus when I'm working on a target. Just in case. It wouldn't do to get caught. Not that what I'm doing is necessarily illegal or anything, just some harmless pranks against guys who more than likely deserve it, but still. Last week, one of the guys wound up dead not long after I saw him. It's a weird coincidence, probably means nothing. Probably some random act of violence. But still...it doesn't sit well with me. Maybe after this last job, I'll give up the business. I have plenty of other work to keep me busy.

When I pull up in front of my mom's house with a trunk full of groceries, Sarah is sitting on the porch swing, waiting for me.

"Finally!" she calls, jumping out of the chair and onto the yellowed lawn. She runs up to my car to meet me at the trunk.

I can't help but notice that her pant legs are getting short. Again. She could almost use them as Capri pants. I buy her new clothes every month, and she grows faster than I can buy them.

"I'm glad I made it in time," I tease her, squeezing her skinny arm. "You're wasting away."

She laughs and wiggles out of my grasp.

I hand her a couple of bags and we bring the food inside.

She grabs some noodles and sauce from one of the bags and puts it out on the counter. I guess that means she's decided what she wants to eat.

While I put stuff away, she pulls a couple of pots and pans out of the cabinet.

"Mom still sleeping?" I ask.

"Yep." She starts the water in the sink and sticks a pot underneath the tap.

I finish putting food in the fridge, and then help her with dinner.

"How is she doing?" I ask while we wait for the water to boil.

Sarah shrugs. "Good, I guess. I haven't seen her much

this week. She's been sleeping a lot, and she was kinda out of it when I got home today."

"It's the chemo. She'll start feeling better in a couple days," I say.

"Yeah, but then she'll just have another round a few days after that." She frowns and turns away from me, opening the package of noodles.

I don't know what to say to that. She's right. And as much as I wish that I could make it better, I can't.

I leave Sarah to the food, grabbing forks and plates and setting the table in the small dining room.

Dinner is ready quickly, and I help Sarah carry the food to the table.

"Should we wake her to eat?" Sarah asks, once we're sitting down.

"Nah, we can save her some leftovers. I'm sure she needs her rest."

Between the chemo and radiation treatments, her sleep patterns have been sporadic at best, not to mention the toll it takes on her body.

I shake the thought away. We're all okay, for now.

"How's school?" I ask while shaking parmesan over my noodles.

"Fine."

"Did you get your homework done?"

"Yep."

"Can you speak in more than one-word answers?"

"Nope." She tosses me a cheeky grin and I shake my head.

"Oh," she says, "I do have some paperwork that needs

to be signed by a parent before tomorrow." She bounds from the table.

I stare at a water spot on the ceiling and listen to her rummaging through some papers on the counter in the kitchen. I'm really glad winter is over and we got through it without having to replace the roof. It's the small things that I have to be thankful for.

She skips back in and hands me a stack of papers.

I shuffle through them. "What is this?"

"Just school stuff," she shrugs.

It's not just school stuff. It's more expenses that we can't afford. Yearbook fees, lab fees, book fees, a fundraiser for the music class...I sigh and rub a hand through my hair. At the bottom of the pile, there's a few more medical bills and a past due notice for the mortgage.

"We need more money, don't we?" Sarah asks.

She must have noticed the pained expression on my face.

I shake my head at her. "It's nothing you need to be worrying about."

"Maybe I could get a job," she says. "I could babysit or something."

"No. You should focus on school. Plus, you need to be here for Mom."

She scowls at me, but she doesn't argue.

I wish she could be a normal kid, with a normal, middle-class childhood. I wish she didn't know about cancer and money problems. I wish I could put her in some kind of sport or something, anything that would help her cope. But we can't afford that.

When she was a baby and I was her age, I enrolled in karate classes at the community center. It was one of the few things in my life that was stable. We had more money then, though. Sarah's dad—my step-dad—was around and he worked and supported us. Money was the only good thing he gave us.

Maybe I can look into something for Sarah to do that isn't too expensive. Maybe the community center still has some classes or activities she can get involved in. She deserves something to look forward to.

I guess I won't be giving up the evil ex business, after all.

4

I strenuously object.

–A Few Good Men

reya

Bethany did a great job setting me up on this date. Mike is cute, nice, smart, funny…everything that anyone could ever want in a guy.

Except I don't want anything to do with him.

The conversation is good and flows smoothly. We talk about school, our families, and our mutual friends. We even talk about the guy they found dead on campus last week, and then right back to less morbid topics.

But then, it happens.

We finish eating. He pays the tab, and we're getting up to leave. He moves forward to give me a hug, and I leap back and stick my hand out to shake.

He seems surprised at first, but then—like the perfect gentleman he is—he smiles and shakes my hand, asking when he can see me again.

"I'll call you," I say.

I won't.

He leaves, but not before offering to walk me to my car, which I politely refuse. Instead, I tell him that I'm going to use the bathroom and he should absolutely not wait for me.

We part ways and once I get to the bathroom I try not to slam my head against the wall.

What is wrong with me? Why can't I find one guy, just *one* that I want to bang?

Once safely locked in a stall, I pull my phone out of my purse and unlock the screen.

"Lucy," I say when she answers the phone.

"This isn't a good sign," she says.

"What isn't a good sign?"

"Your date started less than an hour ago. It didn't go well." Leave it to Lucy to jump right to the point and make logical conclusions.

Lucy and I met about six months ago. She was working in the peer counseling clinic, and I was a hot mess because I caught Cameron cheating on me with Liz the slut. Lucy tried to console me by talking about herpes and cavemen

—which was highly ineffective—but somehow, after that, we became friends.

I should probably mention that Lucy is a genius. And a doctor. And she's just turned twenty-one. It's enough to make even the most ambitious person feel inadequate.

"It went fine. He was fine. He was great, actually...the problem is me."

"You need to give yourself time."

"It's been six months!"

"There's no set time frame required to get over a trauma. Everyone is different. Don't rush yourself."

I hear the door to the bathroom swing open, and someone gets into the stall next to mine.

"You're right," I sigh. Then I change the subject because I'm sick of talking about me. "What are you doing now?"

"I'm at the lab. I'm meeting Jensen at the gallery in about an hour."

Lucy's boyfriend, Jensen, is an amazing artist. He draws these charcoal prints of people that are beautiful and damaged. It's weird that he's all creative and she's all logical. I guess that's why they work.

"Okay. I'll see you tomorrow at breakfast?"

"Yes," she says and hangs up on me.

Typical Lucy conversation.

I exit the stall and start washing my hands. The other person in the bathroom comes out of their stall and starts washing their hands at the sink next to me.

I glance over in the mirror and then have to do a double take.

I recognize the girl next to me, even though she has sunglasses on and she's actually wearing clothes. Unlike last time I saw her, bouncing up and down on my boyfriend.

"Freya," she says when she notices me gaping at her.

"Yep." I didn't think this day could get worse. I was wrong.

Who wears sunglasses inside? Besides Jack Nicholson?

"How are you?" she asks.

"Fine." I yank a paper towel out the dispenser. I have to get out of here.

"I'm glad I ran into you." She slides her sunglasses to the top of her head, over her straight cut black bangs, her gaze pointed at her feet. As soon as the sunglasses are off her face, I realize they were hiding two awful looking black eyes. It must have happened fairly recently because her nose is swollen and I can't help but wonder if someone punched her in the face and why that person wasn't me.

"Oh my God, are you okay?" I ask.

"It's nothing, I was playing softball and I got hit with a ball," she says quickly, shrugging and glancing away from my eyes in the mirror. "Anyway, I wanted to tell you that I'm sorry."

That shocks me into silence. For about three seconds. "You are?" Liz the slut is apologizing?

"Yes. That whole thing with Cameron was a huge mistake. There's no excuse for what I did. An apology at this point is probably useless, but I promised myself if I ever saw you again I would say something."

"Oh."

"So...that's it. I'll see you later," she says quickly, turning towards the door and sliding the glasses back over her eyes.

Liz and I used to be friends. Well, friendly, before the whole Cameron incident. I'd heard stories that she slept around, but she always seemed a little sad and lonely to me, and I can't help but root for the underdog. Plus, she was funny, in a subtle way. Before she tainted my thoughts by her actions, I actually liked her.

The saddest part of the whole thing was that if she hadn't slept with Cameron, we might have been friends.

"Wait!"

She faces me, and I'm confronted with my own reflection in her shiny black sunglasses.

"It's okay," I say. "I know how persuasive Cameron can be, and really, we're both better off without him."

"Tell me about it," she mutters with a small laugh. Then she gets serious. "I've got to go, my brother's waiting for me."

She disappears out the door and I'm left alone.

Damn if this hasn't been the weirdest day of my life. First, I hit someone with my car, then I have a great date that I still manage to ruin, and then Liz the slut apologizes for her slutty ways. I shake my head.

I need to go to bed before anything else happens.

I exit the restaurant, crossing the street to get back to my car. After turning the key in the ignition, I look around carefully before merging into traffic. This day has been bad enough, I don't need any more traffic tickets. Halfway down the street, I see Liz standing next to a small, faded blue Toyota, a guy holding the passenger door open for her.

Must be her brother. They look a lot alike. Same dark hair, same bone structure.

I can't see her eyes since she has the glasses on, but she seems upset. Her brother hugs her as I'm driving by.

It doesn't matter.

I drive past them and head home.

5

The more I know about men, the more I like dogs.

–Gloria Allred

reya

I'm late getting to the restaurant the next morning.

"Hey guys." I plunk down my purse and slide into the booth across from Jensen and Lucy just as he's kissing her on the cheek.

They're so in love, it's disgusting.

"Try not to make me vomit before we eat," I tell them with a groan.

"You have the choice of averting your eyes," Lucy says.

Of course she makes no excuses. Lucy is adorable but she doesn't know it. Well, maybe she knows it, but she doesn't care. She's not really the type to put any stock in appearances. She has long dark hair, wide brown eyes that notice everything and petite features that make her look younger than she is.

"What's the good word, Freya?" Jensen asks.

"There is no good word," I grumble, eyes down on the menu in front of me.

"Still breaking hearts?" he asks with a grin.

"Hardly."

The waitress comes over with her notepad and we order

"What happened last night with your date?" Lucy asks once the waitress is gone.

I groan into my hands and then give them the gory details. I tell them about the wonderful date that I ruined, and what happened with Liz the slut, but I leave out what happened with Dean. I don't know why. I'll tell Lucy eventually, but right now I feel...bad. I'm embarrassed that I hit someone with my car, and too full of guilt so I'm not ready to share yet.

"Tough break, Frey," Jensen says when I've finished the story.

"What about James? The guy who works in the physics lab?" Lucy asks.

She set me up with him last week.

"Oh, you mean the farter."

Jensen's mouth drops open. "The *what*?"

"He farted fifteen times during dinner," I say.

"No," Lucy says, shaking her head. "I don't believe it. You're exaggerating."

"Yes! He did! I counted. And he would yell 'Fore!' after each one."

"No!"

Lucy is aghast, but Jensen is cracking up.

"Yes! I can't make these things up." I lift my hands and let them plop down on the table in a gesture of surrender.

"He doesn't do that at work," Lucy says, her expression concerned. "He seems so normal."

"They all do," I say with a sigh. "But then they come around me and turn into weirdos. And if they're not weird, I am. I'm done with guys, really. No more dates, no more men for me. I think I'm going to be a lesbian." I look at Lucy. "Will you make out with me? I need to see if this will work."

I start to lean over the table with puckered lips, and she pushes me back with a laugh.

Our food arrives and after the server puts down the plates Jensen asks me, "Are you sure you don't want to try again? There's a single guy who has a show this weekend at the gallery and he seems fairly normal."

"No!" I say a little too vehemently. "I mean, it's no big deal. I don't need a man to make me happy. I just need a distraction. A nondate distraction. Something to keep my mind off of, I don't know, everything."

What I really need is something, anything to erase my last, terrible experience with intimacy.

A flash of Dean all hunky and angry flashes in my

mind, and I immediately shove the thought away. That is *not* a helpful distraction.

"So. How've you guys been?" I ask in an upbeat tone, glad to switch the conversation onto them so that I can listen and nod while I stuff my face.

I love food. Food trumps men every time. It's constant and delicious, and hell, you need it to survive. I do not need a man to survive. I just wanted one to erase the pain the last one left behind.

Two days after my breakfast with Lucy and Jensen, I'm walking through campus and heading towards my car. It's a warm day, spring is finally peeking its head onto this side of the world, but despite the beauty of the day and the buds bursting open into pink flowers on trees, I can't help but feel like a turd sandwich.

"You hit him with your car?" Lucy's voice asks in my ear.

I finally got over myself and spilled everything to her. It was only a matter of time.

"Yes," I say into the phone while navigating through people heading the opposite direction through the quad. "It was an accident! I got a reckless driving ticket—my mom is going to love that—and he said he might sue me."

"Have you heard from him since?"

"No. Not a peep. He's letting me simmer in nervous anticipation, the big creep."

"Maybe he won't press charges."

"I doubt that. He told me he would and he was pretty pissed."

"Why don't you just call him and find out?"

"Oh, right," I scoff. "He would love that, me calling to grovel and beg for mercy. No way."

The phone beeps in my ear and I pull it away from my head to see who's calling on the other line. It's a number I don't recognize.

"Luce, I gotta go, I'll call you later," I say and switch to the other line. "Hello?"

"Freya?" It's a male voice.

"Yes?" I'm not sure who this is, but he sounds smoldery.

"It's Dean."

Speak of the devil.

"Oh, hey! Mob guy!" I say. I shouldn't taunt him. Seems like a bad decision since he could be suing me and all, but I just can't control myself.

"Would you quit calling me that? I'm not a mob guy."

"Aww, mob man is grumpy!" I say, like I'm speaking to a child. I start to cheer up. Yes, I'm stuck in a seventh circle of hell, but at least I can make someone else miserable, too.

"Look, I don't have a lot of time. You're pre-law right?" he asks in a low voice, and then continues without waiting for my answer. "I need your help."

That's weird.

"Uh, you realize pre-law is nothing like law school, right? And it's even farther from passing the bar exam and being an actual lawyer. I just take more poli-sci classes than your average student." I hear a strange noise in the background. Like someone on a walkie-talkie.

"Where are you?" I ask.

"County jail."

I stop walking. "Come again?"

"I'm in jail," he says a little louder.

"You didn't have to say it again, I heard you the first time. What are you doing there, they finally bust your gambling ring?"

He makes an annoyed sound into the phone. "No. I didn't know who else to call. I remembered you talking about the law school, and…I used my one phone call on you."

"That was stupid," I scoff.

"Look, they've had me in for questioning all day long. I know they don't have enough to charge me, but I think they're trying to keep me here as long as possible just to be dicks. I need you to help me find out what's going on. I don't have anyone else to ask, and if you help me, I won't press charges for the whole running me over thing."

"Why are they detaining you in the first place?"

There's a pause and I hear someone in the background say, "One minute."

"I don't have time to explain. I'll call you again when they let me go, just promise you'll help me."

"If I promise to help you, you won't sue me?"

"Yes."

"Can I get that in writing?"

"Yes!"

"I don't know, I'm not even sure what I'll be helping you with. What if you want me to do something shady or illegal?"

"Nothing illegal, I promise. I need help with research and legal things."

"But you're in the clink now; how do I know I can trust you?"

"I'm not in the clink," he grinds out. "I'm being held for questioning. They have nothing to charge me with."

"Actually, they could hold you for up to seventy-two hours while the prosecutor works on building a case against you. The cops can't charge you with anything, only the prosecutor can. And if they don't have enough evidence, they can hold you for that entire length of time before they let you go."

He lets out a frustrated groan.

"Time's up," I hear someone say in the background.

"I have to go," Dean says.

He really sounds upset and desperate.

I feel a twinge of guilt in my chest and then I open my big mouth.

"I'll help you," I say quickly. "As a matter of fact, if you drop your case against me, I'll start helping you right now."

"What do you mean?"

"You just sit tight and don't worry. I'll see you soon, sweet cheeks."

There's a shuffle and a click and I'm not sure he heard my last endearment.

Doesn't matter. I shove my phone in my bag while I'm walking, moving quickly towards the parking lot.

I have to go home to change before rescuing Dean. Maybe this isn't the best decision. I mean, I don't *have* to get him out of his current predicament, but if I do, he won't have that whole running-him-over thing to hold over my head so much. I can get myself some leverage and stop feeling so guilty.

This is crazy. I don't even know what he did to get picked up in the first place—what if it's something totally awful? He's sort of a bad boy. I know this. It's why I hired him to beat up Cameron in the first place. I heard he once got in a fight with ten guys and walked away with them all bleeding and collapsed around him, like some fucking superhero.

I throw on the business suit my mom bought me before I started school. I've never worn it because the blazer makes me look like a linebacker, but it'll work for me today. I pull my hair back into a severe knot before racing back out the door to my car.

Here goes nothing.

The county lockup isn't exactly what I expected. It looks more like a sleek office building than a holding for criminals. I walk in as confidently as possible towards the front desk while tossing my hair out behind me before realizing my hair is pulled back and the effect is rather lost.

"I'm here to see my client," I say as haughtily as I can muster although I'm shaking in my sensible heels. I would have loved to wear my stilettos, but they looked more hooker than lawyer. I wanted to look like I belonged on the right side of the bars.

The clerk doesn't even glance up at me. She looks like Nurse Ratched but with a taser instead of the little white cap.

"Name," she barks.

"Freya Morgan, attorney-at-law."

Now her eyes flick up at me. Maybe I should have left out the whole "attorney-at-law" bit. Was that over the top?

"Your client's name?" she asks in monotone.

"Right," I say. "Dean."

Shit. I don't know his last name. I'm lucky I remembered his first name, and didn't call him Thor or Mob guy. My mouth dries and my palms sweat. I'm fucked.

"Dean Collins?" she asks, tapping something into the computer.

"Yes," I say quickly. Dammit, I hope that's him. There can't be that many Deans being held for questioning. Can there? "Dean Collins," I repeat with a nervous swallow.

She gives a brisk nod. "They're in interrogation room C. You've been here before right?"

"Sure. Yes. Of course." If I answer in the affirmative three times, does that make it any less of a lie?

"I'll need your ID."

I take it out and hand it over—hopefully she doesn't look too carefully at the age—and she hands me a guest pass on a lanyard. I put it on over my head and it seems I'm dismissed. I walk around the clerk's counter and down a short hallway. It leads me through a doorway into an office area that's larger than it looked like it would be from the outside. There are quite a few cubicles with people bustling about. A man is cursing at the copy machine. I sidestep him and head towards a few doors along the far wall. There are plaques outside each doorway with names and room numbers. C. Must find C.

It only takes me a few minutes, and then I burst into the interrogation room.

6

The good lawyer is not the man who has an eye to every side and angle of contingency and qualifies all his qualifications, but who throws himself on your part so heartily, that he can get you out of a scrape.

— Ralph Waldo Emerson

Dean

I can't quite believe this is happening to me.

I'm exhausted. The real bitch of it is that I almost didn't take this last job, but when I tried to get out of the gig, the girlfriend offered me double what I normally charge.

The room I'm in is sterile and gray. The detectives have

been questioning me for hours, but I have nothing more to tell them.

We're engaging in yet another staring contest when door swings open, banging against the wall.

Freya marches in.

What the actual fuck?

"Good afternoon." She nods at the detectives, whom I've named Tweedle-dum and Tweedle-dumber because remembering their actual names would humanize them too much, and I prefer to keep people who want me imprisoned in the non-friend zone.

"Mr. Collins is my client. I would like a moment with him, please," she says firmly.

I can't believe she's doing this. She can't get away with it, there's no way they're going to believe—

"Are you aware that your client is being questioned in connection with multiple homicides?" Tweedle-dumber asks her.

Okay, maybe they will believe her. Morons.

I catch the flicker of shock that shoots through her expression when she hears what I'm in for, but she manages to cover it fairly well.

"Of course I'm aware of that," she says.

The detectives stand there and stare at her.

She puts one hand on her hip. "Can I have a moment now, or are there any other asinine questions you wish to attempt to shock me with?"

Once they're gone, she throws herself into the chair across from me and lets out a gusty sigh. "This is like, the most stressful thing, ever," she says.

"What the hell are you doing here?" I don't mean to sound like an ass, but I can't help it. I'm tired. Hungry. Grumpy. And what the hell is she doing? She can't help me if she gets locked up, too.

"Touchy, touchy. I came to bust you out." She straightens up in the seat, the motion pushing her chest out a little and my eyes can't help but be drawn to the movement before I snap them up to her eyes. She has nice eyes. Kind eyes. Big and brown and warm. Like honeyed whiskey.

Jesus, I need to get out of here. The fact I'm having these thoughts about anyone proves that I've seriously lost it.

"You shouldn't have come," I whisper harshly. "You're not a lawyer.

She considers me for a second. "Fine. I can leave if you prefer to be deloused and forced to sleep on a small cot with a large dude named Hank."

I blink at her and try not to crack my teeth as my jaw clenches. I forcibly have to relax. I called her, after all, and she is trying to help me, misguided though her attempt might be. This isn't really what I meant when I told her I needed her help.

"I'm sorry." I scrub at the stubble lining my jaw. "It's been a pretty shitty day."

"I got that from the whole multiple homicide thing, are you kidding me? What the hell happened?"

"Jesse Carmichael," I say, speaking in a low voice.

She shakes her head, but then I see the moment when the recognition hits her and her eyebrows go up so much, they nearly hit her hairline. "The guy that was found dead on campus? They think you killed him? Then what's with the multiple?"

"They found another body this morning, Matt Ellison."

She just stares at me with an odd expression on her face.

I frown at her. "I didn't kill them!"

"Did I say anything? I was just thinking that name sounds familiar, but I'm not sure where I know it from." She taps her lips with her finger.

I don't answer for a moment, watching her thoughts fly across her face. It's one of the things I like about her: you can always tell what she's thinking, and if you can't she'll probably tell you. There's no prevarication. No hiding. So unlike most girls in college. It's one of the reasons I thought of her to call first. Plus the pre-law thing. And I had no one else to call.

"Matt and Jesse..." I swallow, my mouth suddenly dry. "Their girlfriends paid me to knock some sense into them. Ever since you hired me to beat up Kevin—"

"Cameron," she corrects.

"Whatever. Ever since then, beating up exes has become sort of a side business."

"Really? I'm like a trendsetter." This seems to perk her up.

"Yes. I knew this world was full of vengeful bitches, I just didn't realize how many lived within a five-mile radius."

"Are you calling me a vengeful bitch?"

I slowly shake my head. "No. Out of all of them you

were probably the only one I didn't feel any guilt about. Carl is a real asshole."

"Cameron," she corrects again.

"Whatever." I run a hand through my hair. It feels greasy and gross. No time to shower this morning before the cops started knocking at my door. "Anyway, sometime after I left them, *alive and well*," I feel the need to place emphasis on the last three words, "they were both killed. I'm the only suspect, because I'm the only connection they've found between the two."

She watches me as I explain.

"How long have you been here?" she asks.

I shrug. "I don't know. All day. Ten hours, maybe. I told them everything I know, about a million times. They're being pricks because they want to search my apartment, and I told them I want to see the warrant. Since then..." I trail off.

"Why don't you let them search? It might be the easiest way to prove your innocence."

I shake my head again. "There's too much stuff in there. Not necessarily anything that could get me in serious trouble, but maybe some misdemeanor offenses, and...I don't want to incriminate any of my clients. It's not right."

She reaches over and pats me on the hand. "It's sweet that you're concerned about your miscreant ruffian friends," she says before pulling her hand away and standing. "Stay here, I'll be right back." She adjusts her top and visibly straightens before striding back out the door, shutting it behind her.

I almost call out to stop her. What the hell is she going

to do now? But something holds me back. I'm curious to see what she does. She never fails to shock me. One time, I saw her hiding in some bushes in an alley. When I stopped to figure out what the hell she was doing, her hair got caught on some of the brambles and I had to help untangle her.

The odd thing is, I barely remember what her ridiculous excuse was for her behavior. But I do remember how soft her hair felt between my fingers, and how her ass looked sticking up in the air.

I shake my head at the thoughts. I don't have the liberty of indulging in harmless flirtations or coed crushes. I have too many real things to worry about.

A few minutes later, the door flies open again, and Freya is standing there with a goofy grin on her face.

"Let's go," she says.

"Thank you, really. You have no idea," I tell her as I climb into her old VW Bug. The passenger door is busted, so I have to crawl in through the driver's side door.

Freya slides in after me and starts the car.

"No problem. Where am I taking you?" she asks.

"The parking garage next to the language arts building."

We drive in silence for a minute. It's nearly dark outside and her headlights aren't the brightest. Luckily, the road is fairly well lit so she might not hit any small children or animals.

"How did you get them to let me go?" I ask.

She shrugs. "Just a hunch. Everything they have is circumstantial and they're missing something important."

"What's that?"

The side of her mouth tilts as she smiles. "Motive."

We're silent for a moment and then she asks, "Why did you use your one phone call on me?"

It's my turn to shrug. "I didn't know who else to call."

We stop at a red light and I feel her watching me. I keep my gaze focused straight ahead.

"What about one of your buddies from the fights?" she asks.

I shake my head. "I can't ask them," I say. "I need someone who knows something about law. I don't know anyone else connected with the law school, and I can't afford a real lawyer." I turn my head to meet her eyes in the dim light. "I still need your help."

"What kind of help? I'm not anywhere near being a lawyer yet, and until they actually charge you with any crimes—"

"I can't afford to be under this kind of scrutiny and I definitely can't afford bail if they decide to nail me with something. I need to find out who the real killer is, before they charge me with anything."

The light turns green and she slams the gear into place before lurching forward. "You want me to help you find the killer?" she asks, glancing over at me.

"Yeah," I say.

"And this is what you want in exchange for dropping

any case you might have made against me for hitting you with my car?"

"Yeah," I repeat. She doesn't sound like she wants to help and the thought makes me panic, a little. I don't have time for this. I need someone to help me. "Besides, you're the reason I started being a thug for hire in the first place. If you hadn't gotten me into this business, I wouldn't be in this situation."

She frowns and I know I've said the wrong thing.

"It's not my fault you consented when I hired you. You could have said no," she tells me.

"I didn't really have a choice."

"Bullshit. It's not like anyone forced you! I mean, look at you." She eyes me up and down. It takes a while. "And look at me. It's like a snail coercing a mountain."

I wave a dismissive hand in her direction. "All of that's irrelevant. Someone killed these guys. I want to find out who."

"I'm not sure this is the best idea. That's not your job. Or my job. Leave it to the professionals."

"Have you met the cops in this town? They're like the love children of Barney Fife and Chief Wiggum."

"Who's Barney Fife?"

I let out a frustrated moan and plop my head in my hands. I'm getting a headache just thinking about it. "They'll pin this shit on me because they're too incompetent and lazy to find the real killer. I'm an easy solution."

"Okay, well, good luck playing Law and Order." She pulls into the parking lot and stops just inside the entrance, popping off her seat belt and reaching for the door.

I reach out and put a hand on her arm. "Wait, Freya."

"What?" She turns towards me, and then glances down at my hand on her arm, an expression of surprise flitting across her face.

"You don't care that I could sue you?" I ask.

She looks up at me. "You're going to be too busy avoiding a murder charge. I don't think you're going to want to spend more time in court."

I squeeze her arm gently. "Help me. Please?"

"Don't try that playboy charm on me, buddy, I've been burned before and I know better."

I remove my hand and glare at her. "You owe me."

She laughs. "I owe you dick. Plus I just saved you from becoming someone's bitch and learning how to make booze in a toilet. We're square." With that, she shoves out of the car and stands next to the door, waiting for me to get out.

I have to take a deep breath and calm myself down. I don't know why I'm getting so worked up. I mean, I know why I'm upset. I can't have the law breathing down my neck, not when I have to make money to feed my family and keep a roof over their head. Even a leaky one is better than nothing. But I shouldn't be taking it out on Freya. It's not her fault. The fact that she won't help me is bothering more than it should. I just have to think of something to say to convince her. That's all.

When I finally crawl out of the car, Freya is looking at the ground, not meeting my eyes. I stand in front of her and wait for her to look up at me. "It is your fault I started beating up exes in the first place."

"Yes," she says, her hands flapping to her sides in exasperation. "I forced you to take all those jobs. I put a gun to your head. Not to mention, I increased your business and made you more money. How again, do I owe you?"

"Because if you hadn't told all your friends, I wouldn't be facing a murder charge!" I yell.

"Right, you would just be facing illegal gambling and possession with intent to sell charges," she yells back.

"I don't sell drugs," I say, offended.

"Out of all of the insults I give you, *that* one bothers you the most?"

"Whatever." I turn away, running a hand through my hair and stalking off a few paces. "Just forget it. I don't know why I bothered—I thought maybe you had a heart."

I think she says something else, but I don't hear it. I'm walking towards my car. I have too much to worry about to add her to the list.

7

The first step to getting the things you want out of life is this: decide what you want.

–Ben Stein

Freya

Two days later, I can't get Dean out of my head. I'm chased by guilt for not helping him, and every night when I close my eyes, I hear the thump-thump sound his body made when I ran him over.

I should help him.

I don't think he's a murderer. Maybe I'm gullible. A real bleeding heart, but in all of my interactions with Dean, although he's moody and sullen and finds me incredibly annoying, I've never felt scared of him. The guy is ripped. He's all bulging muscles and wide shoulders, if he really wanted to hurt someone (i.e., me, which I'm sure he has) he could, but he doesn't.

Unless he's in the ring. Or being paid. Dammit, okay, maybe I know nothing about him.

I might have been less defensive, I might have even agreed to help him if he had told me he wanted me to help him for an actual valid reason, rather than harassing me into it.

Not that I expected him to say he wanted me to help him because of my keen intellect and cat-like reflexes, I just thought maybe...maybe he would want me to help him because of some actual skill I possessed rather than blame me for his current predicament, or blackmail me into submission.

The one thing that I keep thinking about is the moment he touched me. It was an innocent gesture—he just put his hand on my arm, but for the first time in a long time, I didn't flinch or want to jump away. Instead, I felt a zing of something shoot up my arm and lodge somewhere in my chest.

It's because of his general hotness. Even with his unkempt appearance and tired eyes, he's still way too good-looking. Especially when he put on that mournful, sexy expression. It's my own stupid brain, being attracted to stupid jerks instead of the nice guys. I am such an idiot.

I need someone to talk it over with. Someone logical and understanding. Someone smart, and slightly creepy.

"Lucy!" I bang on her apartment door.

It swings open, and I barge in, throwing myself on her couch.

"Come on in," she says belatedly, shutting the door and joining me in the living room.

"I need your help." I shift over onto my back, flicking my shoes off with the heel of my foot.

"You're so needy," a voice says from the chair opposite me.

"Hey, Ted." Ted's a friend. A very gay friend. His tall, lanky body is draped over Jensen's favorite recliner. "I didn't see you there."

"Obviously." He waves a dismissive hand in my direction.

"Did you need my help as your friend, or my help as a medical professional?" Lucy asks me sitting in the chair next to the couch.

She's not joking, although if you didn't know Lucy like I do, you might mistake that last comment as sarcasm.

"Both," I say. "Ted, you too. I need a male perspective."

"I'm not sure I'm much help in that area," he says.

"Fine, I need the bitchy, irrational perspective."

"That's more like it," he says with relish.

I move my gaze up to the ceiling and frown. "Why does it say 'Get off my sister' on your ceiling?"

Lucy glances up and then shuts her eyes. "Sam," she says. It sounds like a curse word.

"It looks like permanent marker," I say, which doesn't seem to make her any happier.

She shakes her head. "He also printed a life-size color

photo of himself and taped it to the ceiling in our bedroom."

Ted laughs.

Sam is one of her brothers. She has four brothers and they're all crazy and constantly playing pranks on each other.

"I guess that note was left for Jensen. Speaking of, where is Hottie McSexy Pants?" I ask.

"At the studio working on his latest piece. Now tell us what's going on."

I close my eyes and start my story with the whole running-over-Dean thing, since Ted hasn't heard that part yet. I go on and tell her and Ted everything that happened at the jail, and how I totally blew him off.

"Do you want to help him?" Lucy asks when I've finished.

"I don't know. Maybe? I feel guilty for not helping him. Would I feel bad if I was doing the right thing?"

"Let's start with the negatives. What are your reasons for *not* wanting to assist him?" she asks.

"He's too hot. I don't want to be around attractive men. I'm trying to be a lesbian."

Ted snorts. "Worst lesbian ever."

"Fuck off, Ted." I flip him the bird.

"Ouch. The kitten has claws," he says, and then makes a hissing noise.

I can't help but giggle a little.

"Are there any other reasons?" Lucy asks.

"I hardly know him?" I try. "I have better things to do?"

"He's not asking you for a romantic relationship," she points out.

"True," I concede.

"He's not telling you that you can't be a lesbian."

"Also true."

"You were just saying the other day that you wanted a distraction. Doesn't this seem like a great opportunity?" she asks.

"Maybe. I don't know about this guy though. I mean, the detective told me he doesn't have an alibi, and he's their only suspect. What if he is the killer and he's dragging me into his Ponzi scheme?"

"I don't think you understand what a Ponzi scheme is," Ted says. "Why don't we use our little hacker here to do some research on him and see if we can tell if he's a good witch or a bad witch?"

Lucy nods. "That's a good idea, Ted."

Within minutes, her laptop is out and she's typing and reading at an unholy speed. Ted and I are crammed together, looking over her shoulder but trying not to be too annoying about it.

Ted pinches me on the butt.

"Ouch! Hey! What was that for?" I ask.

He shrugs. "You looked like you needed it."

I frown at him, but then Lucy makes a noise.

"Hmmm," she says when her fingers stop moving.

"What is that?" I ask anxiously. "Is that *hmmm* he's a psychopath with a predilection for rolling around naked in rutabagas, or *hmmm* there's nothing?"

"It's an interested hmmm. He's fairly intelligent."

High praise coming from the genius.

She continues, "He graduated high school at the top of his class. He received a near-perfect score on his SATs. He was awarded a full scholarship including a living allowance, but that's when it gets weird. He's living in the apartments up off Center Street."

"The ghetto complex?"

"The plot thickens!" Ted claps his hands together. "With the living allowance and scholarship, he shouldn't have to do the things he does for income. Why spend all that time and effort on the gambling, the fighting, and taking money from the scorned and desperate female population?"

"And he's living in the cheapest place in a ten-mile radius, so what is he doing with the rest of the money?" I ask.

"Inquiring minds want to know." Ted nods at me.

Lucy cranes her neck to meet my eyes. "You know, there's only one way to obtain the answers to these questions."

"I know," I say with a groan. "I have to ask him."

Ugh. Lucy's always so logical and to the point and wanting to take the closest line from A to B.

"But can we eat first?" I ask. "I'm starved."

We order pizza and I force them to talk about themselves to try to get my mind off of the questions circling in my brain.

I'm sitting on the kitchen counter, working on my third slice of pizza pie and listening to Ted gripe about the lack of gay males in the immediate area, while I gripe about his broken gaydar when the front door bangs open.

"Honey, I'm home!"

Jensen bounds into the kitchen and immediately sweeps Lucy into a back-bending kiss.

Ted groans. "God, this is disgusting."

I nudge Ted with my elbow. "You're just jealous." He totally used to have a thing for Jensen. Too bad Jensen's in love with Lucy. And straight. Sort of a deal breaker.

Jensen releases Lucy and grins at us. "Hey guys," he says, snagging a slice of pizza and heading down the hall. "I need to shower," he calls out behind him.

"I do not want to think about that man all naked and slippery in the shower," Ted says.

"You mean, you do, but you know it's wrong."

"Exactly. I'm out of here. Thanks, dollfaces, for the smashing good time." He kisses both of us on the cheek before making a hasty exit.

I slide off the counter onto my feet. "I guess I better get going so you guys can have wild monkey sex."

She smiles at me. "Our sex is way wilder than that of any simian species."

I groan. "I did not need to hear that."

She walks me to the door. "Let me know what happens when you talk to Dean."

I drive home lost in thought. Should I call Dean? What do I say? Do I apologize for being a heinous bitch? He wasn't exactly Mr. Politeness when I got him out of jail, but he did, admittedly, have a better reason for being in a bad mood than I did.

I'm so absorbed in my own thoughts that I miss the turn off to my apartment. Dang it.

I flip around at the next street and turn back in the right direction. There's a car behind me, but they seemed to be turning down the road I used as a U-turn. No wait, the headlights behind me swing around after I do and continue to follow along behind me.

That's weird.

Am I being followed? It wouldn't be the first time. I have a tendency to drive...ahem, aggressively, and piss people off.

I make a few quick and random turns but the car stays fairly close behind. I try to get a read on the license plate, but the headlights are shining into my eyes through the rearview mirror, and I can't even tell what kind of car it is.

Now I'm getting nervous. I really don't want to park in the most likely empty parking lot in front of my small building, and walk in with this potential weirdo slash murderer trailing behind. I head away from my house and towards the nearest police station.

I drive into the parking lot and my stalker takes off down the street, no longer following. I still don't get a look at the type of vehicle they were driving, or the license plate number or anything. I park in an empty spot and wait until my speeding heart calms down.

I really need to take more care while I'm driving so I don't anger vigilante drivers. Or run people over.

I pull my cell phone out of my purse and find Dean's number. I have him listed as *Mob guy*.

"Hello," he answers gruffly.

"Dean," I say. "It's Freya."

There's a pause and then, "Yeah?"

"Um." I really should have thought this through more. What am I going to say?

"I'm sorry," I blurt out.

There's silence. It goes on and on and starts to edge into the realm of awkward.

"Hello?" I say, slightly exasperated.

"I'm here," he says.

"And you have absolutely nothing to say to that?"

"I'm just surprised is all."

"Surprised about what?"

"Surprised about a lot of things." He's quiet again, but this time I can hear him moving. I imagine him pacing around his apartment. Maybe he's wearing a tight-fitted tank top—oh wait, that's way too effeminate looking. Maybe he's shirtless. And he's just finished lifting weights so he's all sweaty and his pecs are glistening in the light...

Oh, God. I need to stop. I do *not* like him. He's a suspected murderer with secrets the size of Cleveland, and I do not want to think of him that way!

"Surprised that you called," he says, finally. I was so lost in how not attracted to him I am, that I nearly forgot he was on the phone. "Doubly surprised that you apologized. You didn't do anything wrong, Freya."

"I didn't?"

"No. I don't blame you for not wanting to help me. I was

grasping at straws. I don't know why I thought of you. I'm sure you have better things to do with your time, and we really don't know each other."

Those were my thoughts exactly, but hearing him say them sort of irks me.

I rub my thumb over a worn spot on my steering wheel and take a breath before asking, "Don't you have a friend, or a girlfriend that can help?" I ask. Too obvious?

"I don't have time for friends."

Hmph. He totally dodged my not-so-discreet jab at information on his love life.

"Well. If you still want me to help you out of the whole murder suspect thing, I suppose there's a few things I can do." I let out a gusty sigh just so he knows how much he's putting me out.

"Really?"

That perks him up.

"Really," I say. "Can you meet me at my place tomorrow? My last class gets out at three fifteen."

"I can be there at three forty-five," he answers quickly.

"Perfect," I say. "And bring any information you have about the victims."

I give him my address and then we hang up.

I immediately dial Lucy.

"Hey, my little research muffin, can you do me a huge favor?"

8

*ou've got to look on the bright side, even if there ain't one.*

—Dashiell Hammett

Dean

I make it to Freya's apartment right on time. I would have been a little earlier, but I had to stop after class and get a haircut because I was beginning to look like a homeless street urchin.

Not that Freya will care. I looked like hell the last time she saw me, and she didn't seem to notice. Not that I care if she cares, anyway...dear God, I'm starting to sound like a woman.

I jog up the steps to her door and rap out a brisk knock, surprised when my heart seems to accelerate and my stomach twists. I wrap my hands around the backpack straps on my shoulders and take a deep breath.

Am I nervous?

The door swings open and she's standing there, perfectly coiffed, with a shirt that's a little bit low cut and a skirt that's a little too short.

"Hey," she says, and I swing my gaze back to her face.

"Hey," I say, and my voice cracks on the word. I clear my throat. What is wrong with me? I have a mother and a sister; I know better than to ogle. But for some reason with her it's like I can't control it. She's petite, but perfectly proportioned.

I don't feel too bad because it seems like she's been checking me out, too, and for a brief moment I'm glad I got cleaned up before coming over.

She steps back to let me in and I follow her inside and into the living room.

"Your place is...interesting," I say.

It looks like the Brady Bunch threw up in here. Everything is seventies style colors and patterns. There's an orange couch, a yellow recliner and a chair decorated in embroidered flowers.

She sits on the sofa, grabbing a laptop off the coffee table.

I sit gingerly on the flower-covered chair next to her.

"My mom owns a store with a bunch of vintage stuff," Freya explains before getting right to business. "Did you bring the info you have?"

I open my bag. I wrote down as much as I could remember during class this morning. I hand her the crumpled paper.

She gives me a pointed look. "Really?"

I shrug.

"This looks like it's been ripped out of a notebook and scribbled on by a three-year-old," she says.

I don't say anything, and she rolls her eyes.

After looking it over, she asks me to translate a few words. Then there's silence while she types stuff into the computer.

I have nothing to do but watch her. She bites her bottom lip while she's thinking. I wonder what it would be like to bite it for her. I shut my eyes, like that will quell the thought. It's been too long since I've been with a girl. I'm sure that's all it is.

"I'm putting this information together with the information my friend Lucy gave me. It's not much. She's still working on cracking into their files. She's sort of a computer wiz," she tells me, forcing me to open my eyes.

She finishes typing and then reads the information aloud. "Victim number one was Jesse Carmichael. He was an English major, a part of the wrestling team, and a member of Sigma Alpha Epsilon fraternity, where he also lived. He was dating Daisy McHenry who hired you to give Jesse a giant wedgie...really?"

She glances over at me and I clear my throat.

"After I beat up Conrad for you—"

"Cameron," she interjects in monotone.

"I didn't want to commit any further violence. I typically agree to embarrass or frighten the evil exes, but beyond that…" I shrug.

"Okay," she says. She sounds surprised. I'm glad for it. My business depends on people believing I'm more of a badass than I actually am.

"Well," she says, "I'm glad I hired you before your conscience kicked in." She tosses me a bright smile before continuing. "Victim number two was Matt Ellison. He was majoring in biochem, was not involved in any campus activities, lived in White Pine," the cheapest dorms on campus, "and was dating Samantha Ferguson. She hired you to pretend like you were going to chop off his member, but then let him go once he started crying. Both victims were shot at close range with a nine millimeter—in the head. Both bodies were found on campus, one outside of the library and the other in a bathroom in the sports and rec building." Her eyes roam over the screen, like she's looking for something more. "There's no connection we could find between the two victims. Except you."

I lean my head back against the chair. "So what's next?"

She taps a finger on her lips and thinks for a moment before responding. "I'll find Daisy and Samantha, ask them some questions, see if they cough up anything good. You go to the frat house and maybe check with the families. Ask some questions about who they hung out with, who might want to kill them. See if there's a connection somewhere that we missed."

"Okay." I nod, grateful that there's at least a plan. I'm not sure I should approach the girlfriends since they're the ones who hired me, so that seems like a wise decision.

We're silent for a moment. She's staring at the computer screen and I'm staring at her.

"Why don't you have an alibi for either night?" she asks suddenly, shifting her gaze to mine. "The detective mentioned it when I was at the jail."

I wonder if she doubts my innocence, but then again, she is helping me, and she asked me straight up instead of being secretive or weird about it, which I have to appreciate.

"Both nights, it was late by the time I left campus. I went straight home."

"Oh. That makes sense." She nods and then gazes back at the computer for a minute, seemingly lost in her own thoughts.

I clear my throat and her eyes snap to mine.

"Thank you," I say.

"No problem." She waves a hand at me.

"No really." I lean forward in the chair, resting my elbows on my knees. "The whole thing is so overwhelming, I didn't even know where to start. It was like a mental wall. I feel better now, knowing there's at least a plan of some sort."

She nods. "Are you hungry?" she asks suddenly.

"I could eat."

She grins at me. "I can *always* eat."

We go to a fifties-style diner down the street. She gives me a strange look when I open the door to my old beat-up Subaru for her. I guess she's not used to that, but my mom taught me how to treat a lady, which includes opening doors and carrying heavy things. It might be old school, but far be it from me to question my mom.

After we order, and the waitress brings our drinks—iced tea for her and Coke for me—she starts in with questions.

"So. How's the life of frivolous gaming and gratuitous violence been treating you?"

I stick the straw in my drink and fiddle with the paper wrapper on the table. "It's good for now. But I'm sure that will change once word gets out that I'm being observed in connection with two homicides."

"Will that be a big burden?"

I shrug and keep my eyes on the table. I feel like she's digging for information—she's not a very good interrogator—so to keep my hands busy, I grab my straw wrapper and begin folding it together with hers.

Apparently, my silence isn't enough of a clue.

"Why do you do all that stuff, anyway?" she asks.

"For the money," I answer, giving her a look that says, *duh*.

"Why not just get a job?" she persists.

"Because I'm a full-time student and my frivolous gaming pays about quadruple what I would get working part-time at Starbucks."

"But—"

"Look," I interrupt before she tries for more. "I don't know what you're after with this line of questioning, or why you're suddenly so interested in my finances, but I'm not telling you anything." I drop the straw wrappers and cross my arms over my chest.

She bites her lip and looks a bit chagrined.

Good.

"Fine," she grinds out.

Her mollified tone amuses me. I flash her a quick smile.

"What about you?" I ask.

"What about me?"

"How are you living in the lap of luxury? You have a job?"

"I had savings from my high school job, money from graduation, and I work for my mom at her shop in the summers. I also offer a transcription service occasionally to a law firm in town. That's how I pay my rent and for food and stuff. My mom pays my tuition."

"Ah," I say.

"See?" she says, pointing a finger at herself. "Open book."

I lean toward her, elbows on the table. "Are you suggesting that I'm not an open book?"

She makes a derisive noise. "You're like the Great Wall of China."

"Am I?"

"You've got walls so big, they can see them from space."

I have to chuckle at that. "Maybe."

Our food arrives. We both ordered cheeseburgers. There's silence for a moment while we dig in, but it's not uncomfortable.

After a minute of watching her eat in between my own bites, I have to say something. "Wow, you can really eat."

She finishes chewing a bite before responding. "Yep."

"No really, I've taken two bites and you're already

halfway done. You just like, unhinged your jaw, and shoved the food in there. How'd you do that?"

"It's a special talent."

"It really is."

She finishes her food, and then I catch her eyeballing my fries.

I shake my head and nudge the plate in her direction. "I can't believe you ate all of that and you're still hungry."

"I love fries," she says with way too much feeling.

For a fleeting moment, I wonder if I could get her to be that emotional about me, but I quickly dismiss the thought.

"Do you have a tapeworm?" I ask.

She just snorts and keeps eating.

After we're done, she tries to pay her half, but I can't let her, despite my financial situation.

"Consider it a thank you for the time you've spent helping me," I tell her.

I drop her off in front of her apartment and she goes over the plan one final time. I'm going to find the family and friends of the victims, and she'll track down the girlfriends.

"You know what we need right now?" She turns towards me before getting out of the car, her hand on the door.

"What's that?"

"The *Law and Order* sound, you know, the clank-clank between scenes. That would happen and then the camera would pan to me interviewing the girls."

I can't help but laugh, and then I shake my head. "You've got problems, you know that?"

9

There are some people who still feel threatened by strong women. That's their problem. It's not mine.

—Gloria Allred

Freya

CLANK-CLANK!

I find Daisy, Jesse's girlfriend, er, widowed girlfriend, after her one o'clock class gets out. Lucy was able to obtain both girls' class schedules. She's the best stalker ever.

"I've already told the police everything I know." Daisy tells me after I approach her and ask what she knows about Jesse's death. She stopped to talk to me when I walked up, but after my Mariska Hargitay impersonation and invasive questions, she started moving. Now I'm following her through crowded halls trying to catch her answers over the buzz of noise. Daisy looks like her name: blonde hair, blue eyes and flowing bohemian clothing.

"And that is?" I ask.

She shoves open the door to outside and doesn't hold it open for me even though I'm walking behind her. Rude.

"Jesse left the library late that night. He texted me before he left, and then I texted Dean."

"You were still in contact with him even though you guys broke up?"

"I pretended to forgive him and make friends so I could exact my revenge." She darts through a crowd of students yelling and holding signs outside the administration building—they're protesting something about the college using athletic materials made by blind orphans in China—but I'm hot on her heels.

"Did your revenge involve death and dismemberment?"

This stops her. We're still outside, between the administration building and the library. It's a bright spring day and the sun brings out the horror in Daisy's eyes at my question.

"Of course not!" Her eyes dart around to see if anyone is listening. "I wasn't even around that night. I was at a friend's house with three other witnesses. Unlike some people I have an alibi. And that's all I know, okay?" She shrugs her bag up more firmly on her shoulder. "Dean texted to tell me the deed was done. I didn't think he was going to kill the guy."

I really don't like how she keeps trying to throw Dean under the bus, and how defensive she is. It makes me more suspicious of her.

"He didn't," I say.

"I wouldn't be so sure."

"What time did Dean text you?"

She rolls her eyes but pulls her cell phone out of a side pocket in her bag and scrolls through it.

"Ten twenty-seven," she says.

I write the information down. If the coroner nailed down a time of death, that might be useful.

"Did Jesse have any enemies?"

She shakes her head. "Not that I know of."

CLANK CLANK!

Samantha, victim number two's ex-girlfriend, is a music major. I catch up with her before her violin practice outside the orchestra room. She's tall and thin with long brown hair and a pinched expression.

"Can I ask you a few questions about Matt?" I ask.

Her eyes widen and then she bursts into tears and runs away.

Well, that was useful.

A few days after my unsuccessful attempt at being Veronica Mars, Bethany forces me out for a girls' night.

I definitely need it. I haven't had a chance to tell Dean what I learned (or didn't learn). I tried to call him yesterday, but he didn't answer. Maybe he's still working on getting his side of the information. I hope he finds something.

Part of me feels like I should be more cautious around him. I mean, I'm being pretty trusting considering he's connected to two homicides, and he doesn't have an alibi. But I believed him when he said he went straight home to go to bed. It was late at night in the middle of the week.

Unless he doesn't have an alibi because he really is the killer, and he's luring me into a false sense of complacency by being all hot and smoldery, and then he's going to take me to his evil lair and have his wicked way with me.

Wait. This isn't sounding so bad.

The first thing I see when Bethany leads me through the door to the hot new hangout downtown is Cameron sitting at the bar.

"No," I say immediately, stopping in my tracks. "I can't go in there."

Ted runs into my back and then puts his arm around me. "Lady, chill, we will protect you from the heathen. You need a night out. He won't even see you in this crush. Now scoot that fine ass in there before we piss off the people behind us."

I glance over my shoulder. I see Ted's patient expression, and behind him a mob of people waiting in line. He's right. This isn't a huge town, and I can't hide from Cameron forever. I can, however, go in there and have a good time and completely ignore him.

"Come on, beyotch." Bethany grabs my hand, looping it through her arm, and tugs me into the crowded space.

The new bar is nice, with brick walls and bar height tables littering the spaces around the bar. There are a few pool tables on one end and a stage at the other for live shows. There's no show tonight though, just light music filtering in the background, almost completely overcome by the noise of the crowd.

I can't believe I agreed to go out tonight, but I thought it would help take my mind off other things. Too bad *other things* is at the bar, eyeballing me through the crowd.

We manage to find a table and order drinks, and Ted's right, within minutes I've almost forgotten that my evil ex is present.

"That one's totally gay," Ted says, nodding to a guy bending over the pool table.

"No way," Bethany says. "Your gaydar is the worst. He does have a nice ass though; maybe I should take him home tonight. Wait...maybe you should take him home tonight." She pats me on the arm.

I love Bethany, I really do, but she's trying to turn me into a major slut.

"I'm not taking anyone home."

"Why not? I thought that was the whole point of coming here!"

"I thought the whole point of coming here was to hang out with my friends, not shack up with some gay dude."

"He's so not gay," she insists.

"Wait!" Ted slams his hand on the table. "There's an app for that." He pulls out his smartphone.

"There's a gay app?" Bethany asks incredulously.

"Yep. You take a picture of someone and upload it and it tells you if they're gay or straight. It's called *Let There be Gay*."

"Okay, that can't be accurate," I say.

Bethany has already pulled out her phone and she takes a picture of Ted while he's looking at me. "It doesn't work," she informs us. "It says you're *straighter than arrow that's been rammed up an elephant's ass*."

"It does not, you ignorant slut!" He makes a grab for her phone and she pulls it just out of reach.

"It also says that you have a tiny penis and man boobs."

Ted gasps and stops grabbing at Bethany in order to splay his hand on his chest. "Ouch. That hurt."

"Awww." Bethany pats him on the shoulder. "You're sensitive today. Are you manstrating?"

He snatches her phone away. "Ha!" he says, fiddling with her phone and then frowning down at it. "Hey. This isn't even working!"

"I know." She smirks. "The battery died like a half hour ago. It's time for an upgrade."

"You are such a whore," he says, handing her phone back.

"Truth." She nods in agreement.

"I gotta pee," I say.

"Overshare much?" Ted grimaces at me and rolls his eyes.

"Anyone else have to go?"

"Ugh," Bethany says, waving me away. "The lines to the ladies are the worst. I'll go later. You know how it is: if you pee at the beginning of the night, you'll have to go every fifteen minutes for the rest of it."

I finish the last sip of my martini and head through the crowd towards the restrooms in the back. I've just passed the bar when Cameron appears in front of me.

Mother fucker.

I try to edge around him without saying anything, but he stops me with a hand on my shoulder. I jerk away from his touch.

"Hey, girlie, how've you been?" he asks, giving me a charming smile that shows his dimple.

"Great." I try to step around him again, but there's too many people in the way and he mimics my movement and intercepts.

He's standing too close. I work on not flinching and try to quell the nausea rising in my stomach. If I thought my reaction was bad around most guys, around Cameron it's a million times worse. I clench my fists at my sides to stop them from shaking.

"You should let me buy you a drink," he says.

"No, thanks."

"Come on, don't be like that." His voice is placating, almost nervous sounding.

If I didn't have first-hand knowledge of his douchbaggery, this might be convincing.

"I know we didn't end on the best of terms—"

"Cameron," I interrupt him. "It's been over between us for a long time. I wanted monogamy and you wanted to screw anything with a pulse." I swallow the urge to mention the other part of why I hate his guts. He doesn't see it the way I do, and I don't want to talk about it in a crowd. Or at all, really. "It's no big deal. I'm over it, okay? Have a nice life."

I step around him again, and this time he lets me pass.

There's a huge line to the ladies room but by the time I get in there and finish, there's only a couple people left in the line.

"Figures," I mutter. I should have waited like Bethany.

Wading my way back through the crowd, I groan out loud when Cameron stops me again, this time by the bar.

"Hey," he says. "Look, I just want to be friends," he says, holding up his hands in a gesture of supplication that I don't believe for a minute.

"I don't want to be your friend," I say.

"That's fine," he says. "Just let me buy you one drink, and I'll leave you alone."

"Nope." I shake my head. There's no way I'm opening that door.

He smiles his old, charming smile that made me fall for him all those months ago. Now it just makes me want to throw angry kittens at him.

I turn around, not even bothering to try stepping around him and head the long way around back to the table. The bar is super crowded, but I need a drink.

I catch a glimpse of Liz the slut in the crowd near the bar, and I move quickly away. Dear Lord, what is it with this town? Why couldn't I live somewhere with millions of people so I don't have to worry about running into the last two people on the planet that I want to see?

I wonder—very briefly—if she's here with Cameron, and I'm almost surprised to discover that I don't care.

Eventually, I find a small empty spot and order a beer on my way back to Ted and Bethany.

When I get there, Ted is gone and there's a couple of guys I don't know sitting with Bethany.

"Where's Ted?" I ask when I hop onto the chair next to her.

"He left to hook up with some dude from his English class," she says with a shrug, and then nods towards the guys at the table. "This is Devon and Colton."

"Hi," I wave. Devon is tall with dark hair and dark eyes. Colton is the one with the nice ass that Ted thought was gay.

"I think I'm going to finish this drink and head home," I tell her.

"No!" She pouts. "You have to hang out with us." She leans a little closer and whispers in my ear. "I was right, he's not gay! I think he might actually like me! And his friend is cute, too." She pulls back and winks at me.

I look over at this allegedly cute friend. I guess he's okay. I should be attracted to him—I generally like the tall dark and handsome type—but I'm just feeling...meh. As usual.

Bethany doesn't seem to notice my disinterest. She grins at me, and then Colton whispers something in her ear. She giggles and turns in his direction.

Devon tries to have a conversation with me, but it's just

the same old, same old. What's your major? Where are you from? Etcetera, etcetera.

We reach an awkward pause, and he says, "I gotta take a piss." Then he belches. Loudly. And walks away.

Sigh.

Colton and Bethany left the table at some point and I'm not sure where they went, so I'm now sitting alone. I glance around the bar, sip my beer, and people watch. Inevitably, my eyes run over Liz the slut again.

She's at the bar with a couple of other girls I vaguely recognize, and they're sitting only a few seats down from Cameron the creep. I must stare a little bit too long, because her eyes meet mine and she gives me a half-smile.

I smile back but then look quickly away, hoping she'll get the hint that I don't want her to come over and chit chat.

After taking a small sip of my drink, I risk another glance. Damn it, she's heading this way.

I stare down into my half-empty glass but it doesn't have any of the answers to life, the universe, and everything.

"Hey," Liz yells over the crowd, sidling up to the table, a little too close, totally infiltrating my bubble. Her face looks better than the last time I saw her. The bruising has faded into a mottled yellow, and she's made a valiant attempt to cover it up with makeup. If I didn't already know it was there, and if I were farther away, I might not notice.

"Hi."

"How's it going?" she asks.

"Fine."

This isn't uncomfortable *at all.*

"Did you see who's here?" she asks, nodding in the direction of the bar.

I glance over, even though I know exactly who she's talking about, but I don't see him anymore. Maybe he went home.

"Yep," I say anyway.

"Kinda weird right? All of us in the same place at the same time..."

Dude. What is wrong with this chick? Is this conversation necessary?

"Um...yeah. Weird."

"Ladies."

Oh, dear God, kill me now.

Cameron is standing between us, way too close. I thought Liz was in my bubble, but Cameron can probably count my eyelashes from this distance.

At least Liz looks as ill as I feel.

She steps away from the table and says, "I've gotta go see my friends." And then she's gone so fast, I'm surprised she didn't leave a Liz-shaped cloud behind like the roadrunner.

"Looks like it's just the two of us," Cameron says, with a half-smile that would likely be considered sexy by those who didn't know the real him.

"I've gotta take a piss." I don't. I slide off the chair, maybe a little too eager to get away from him, and knock my purse off the back of the seat in the process. I do not want to bend over with Cameron standing there staring at me, so I awkwardly squat straight down and grab it.

When I stand, he's still there.

I down the last half of my beer and then slam the glass on the table. I don't say anything else, just head back to the bathroom. I'm surprised Cameron doesn't say anything or try to stop me.

It's nearly empty, just one person in a stall, so I put my purse on the counter and dig out my phone. I'll call Bethany and have her rescue me—there's no way I'm leaving this place without an escort since Cameron doesn't seem to be getting the hint.

I dial her number and it immediately goes to voicemail.

Shit. She told Ted her phone was dead.

Now what?

The toilet flushes and a girl with tattoo-covered arms and a sun dress emerges, giving me an odd look before she washes her hands and leaves.

I play on my phone for a minute while I consider my options, checking out various social media apps and my e-mail. A couple more ladies come in to use the facilities and then leave, and I'm alone once again.

Okay. Maybe I've waited him out and I can leave without being accosted. Maybe I should call Lucy.

Hmm. My brain is starting to feel...fuzzy. That's weird.

Lucy. Luuucy. Weird word, Lucy. If I say it enough times it loses all meaning, Lucy, Lucy, Lucy...

I turn on the sink and splash some water on my face. I'm getting super tired all of a sudden, and I feel ill. Did I eat something bad? Oh God, I have to puke.

I stumble into a stall and then everything goes black.

I don't know how long the blackness lasts. It could be

minutes, it could be hours. I come to some time later on the bathroom floor, my face pressed against cold, dirty tile. What is happening? My purse is strapped to my body. I dig through it, fumbling for my phone.

I have to call someone. I was going to call someone before, but I can't remember who.

Lucy.

I can call Lucy.

It takes forever to find her name in my phone. My fingers feel like sausages that aren't linked whatsoever to my body and I think I black out again momentarily.

I come to again, still in the bathroom. This time, I'm lying in vomit. Is that my vomit? Did I puke? I don't remember. My phone is still clutched in my hand. I have like a million missed calls and they all say Lucy. Did I call her? Did we speak? I have no idea. I still feel dizzy and out of it, but I think the vomiting must have helped because I'm able to get up and stumble out of the stall to the bathroom sink.

A chick with about fifty piercings in her face and bright blue eye shadow looks at me with a scrunched face. "You look like shit, girl."

"There are two of you," I slur.

She laughs. "I bet there are. You okay?"

"Fine, I think," I say. I splash water on my face and when I look up again, she's gone. Did I imagine that entire conversation? I'm seriously tripping. I need to go home. Find someone or call a cab or something. Shit.

Somehow, I make it outside although I don't actually remember walking back through the bar. The cool night air feels great on my face. Maybe I can find my car and pass out. Wait. Did I drive?

"Freya, are you okay?" Cameron's suddenly in front of me, all concerned eyes and touchy-feely hands.

"No," is all I can manage.

Inside, I'm screaming, *No, no, no, no*. I don't want him here, I don't want him touching me, it makes me remember the last time he touched me and it was baaad.

He puts his arm around my waist. "Let me take you home," he says.

"No," I say again.

"You're clearly not in your right mind. What did you drink tonight? Did you take something?"

"No."

"Let me help you." He starts guiding me down the street, away from the lights of the bar and the people. Panic swells in my veins, but I'm still too out of it to pull away. It's like one of those dreams where you can't yell no matter how hard you try, and you feel like you're walking in quicksand

Then a voice emerges from the darkness. "I've got her from here."

I know that voice. Someone is pulling me away from Cameron.

I turn and Dean is towering over me. I nearly weep with relief.

"Who the fuck are you?" Cameron asks. He does not sound happy.

"I'm her boyfriend. Who the fuck are you?"

"Boyfriend?" I ask, confused.

The ground disappears underneath me, but no, that's just Dean lifting me into his arms like I weigh no more than a toddler. Of course, compared to him, I am approximately the size of a toddler so there is that.

"It's okay," he murmurs into my hair.

I relax into him. He smells so good. Much better than the stank coming from…um I think that's me.

I glance over at Cameron, but he's turning away. I think I glimpse a flash of something in his face—anger, frustration—but I'm tired and dizzy and I'm probably just imagining things.

"I'm so dizzy," I say.

"I know," he says and it's probably the gentlest tone I've ever heard coming out of his mouth. This is like a dream. It's like Dream Dean. I like him much better than grumpy mob guy.

"I don't understand…" I start, but then it all goes black again.

10

*obody can hurt me without my permission.*

–Mahatma Ghandi

Freya

I wake up in a strange bed. It's comfortable. Clean. Smells good. The sheets are soft. Smells like...a man. Oh God, what have I done? I bolt out of the bed and immediately feel both dizzy and cold. I look down. I'm in my bra and panties. Nothing else. And not my cute panties, but the ones reserved for laundry day and that one week each month where no one is getting near me anyway.

Holy shit.

What the fuck.

Am I still drunk?

There's a digital clock on the bedside table. It's almost noon.

Dean appears in the doorway, making me jump. "You're awake," he says.

I stare at him. How the hell did I get here? What happened last night? Did we…?

"Where's my clothes?" I ask in a strangled voice instead of what I want to ask because I chicken out at the last second, and I'm not sure I want the answers to those other questions.

"I had to take them off. You threw up all over them." He shoves his hands in his pockets and won't meet my eyes, focusing on the ground directly in front of him.

"They're in the dryer," he says after a moment of silence. "I'll get them."

He leaves and it hits me that I'm standing next to his bed half naked.

Dammit, no wonder he wouldn't look at me. I quickly get back under the covers. If I was puking last night, that means I wasn't fornicating. This is a good thing. Embarrassing as hell, but good. The last thing I want is to replace my last horrible memory of sex with…nothing. Drunk black-out sex. Ugh.

Dean returns with my clothes in hand, and I sit up, clutching the sheet to my chest even though it's way too late for such formalities.

"If you want to shower," he says, not meeting my eyes, "the bathroom is just through there." He points at the door to the side of the bed, offering me an embarrassed smile and a slight blush, which is actually sort of adorable considering he's normally all calm, cool, collected and generally pissed off. He leaves the folded pile of my clothes at the bottom of the bed before disappearing out the door again, shutting it gently behind him.

As soon as he's gone, I roll over and scream into the pillow.

Then, I very calmly walk into the bathroom, take care of my basic needs, and shower for a good twenty minutes. I use his shampoo and body wash which smells like boy, and I probably enjoy that a little too much. I squeeze some of his toothpaste into my mouth and swish, and then I get dressed. Thank God I wore something normal and not super slutty last night: a pair of skinny jeans and a nice top that's only slightly hookerish due to the amount of cleavage on display.

I exit the bathroom and take a moment to look around his room. It's clean and simple. His bed sits on a simple metal frame. The walls are plain white. There's a small brown dresser in the corner, and a narrow wood desk with a small black laptop lying shut on top.

Leaving his room, I discover the rest of his apartment is small, but like his bedroom, modest and clean. Except for the bajillions of locks on the door and the camera in the entryway.

Dean is sitting on his sofa. It's obvious he slept there the night before. There's a pillow and a neatly folded blanket next to him.

I sit gingerly on the opposite side of the couch and ask, "What happened?"

"Your friend Lucy called me last night and asked me to get you at that bar. Apparently, you called her in a drunken stupor, and she couldn't get a hold of the friends you should have been with. She didn't have a car, and she was worried it would take her too long to get to you. I'm still not sure how she found my number."

I smile. "She's good at things like that."

"When I got there," he continues, "that douchebag Clarence—"

"Cameron," I interrupt.

"Whatever. He was hauling you off somewhere. I intervened and brought you back here. You were totally passed out the entire way, and then once I got you up the stairs, the projectile vomiting began."

I cringe. "I'm so sorry," I say.

"I really thought I was gonna have to bust out the Latin chants and holy water."

I laugh, because if I didn't, I would probably cry. "Well, I'm glad it didn't come to that."

"How much did you drink?" he asks.

"Not enough to turn into Pukey McGee." I lean back on the couch and close my eyes, reliving the night in my mind. "We got there, ordered drinks, I had a martini. I went to the bathroom, but then I ran into Cameron and—"

"Conner bought you a drink?"

I open my eyes and turn my head towards him, still leaning back against the couch.

"Cameron," I correct although I know he does that on purpose. "And no. I bought myself a beer and drank it back at the table far, far away from him. Although…" I trail off, remembering the rest of the night.

"What?" Dean asks quietly after a minute.

"He came over when I was about halfway through the glass."

"He had access to your drink." His eyes are narrowed and pointed straight at me.

What did I do now? What happened to the nice, blushing Dean who brought me my clothes and averted his eyes when confronted with my half-naked body?

"No." I shake my head. I know exactly what he's insinuating. "Not possible." I don't really believe that Cameron spiked my drink, and yet a chill races over my entire body.

"He roofied you," Dean says, crossing his arms over his chest and glowering at the coffee table in front of us like the inanimate piece of cheap furniture is the cause of all his woes.

"No," I say again.

"The alternative is that you drank a twelve pack you forgot about."

"But," I sigh. "I had control of my glass the whole time!" Except for when I was leaving and dropped my purse and had to crouch down to retrieve it.

I'm in full denial mode outwardly, but inwardly, I think hard about that moment. The moment I had my back to him. He had opportunity, sure, but who in the world keeps roofies up their sleeves?

It's a stupid question. Of course Cameron would do something like that, he's the Titanic of douchecanoes, I know this.

"No," Dean says, shaking his head. "He could have done it without you noticing. That bar was packed. It just takes a second of distraction."

He's right and I hate that he's right. It's really not that much of a stretch. I'm more embarrassed that I was stupid enough to have a drink in an open container in Cameron's general vicinity. The sadistic bastard probably wanted to get me loaded so he could do what he wanted to me. The thought makes me shiver and a frisson of panic runs down my spine. The memory of Cameron on top of me flips through my brain. I try to shove the memory back, but I can't. Normally, I excel at repressing those memories and shoving them way, way down. I'm emotionally healthy like that, but right now I'm too tired and hungry and maybe still a little buzzed.

"Hey," Dean says. And then he does something I never would have expected from the giant brute: he pulls me into him. Right over the blanket and pillow between us, sending the items bounding to the floor.

I'm shaking, and my breath is leaving my body in panicked bursts. How freaking awful is this. It's bad enough that I puked my guts out all over him, now I'm having a giant meltdown like a sissy la-la.

He's so big and bulky, a look I never thought I would appreciate on a guy, but with Dean it works. There's lots of muscle under that T-shirt and I'm getting the pleasure of feeling them with my hands tucked between us and his chest under my cheek since I'm sitting in his lap.

Oddly enough, thinking about Dean's muscles distracts

me from my thoughts of Cameron, instead of reminding me of him—like what usually happens with guys.

"It's okay," he says after a moment. "Nothing happened."

The rumble of his voice in his chest is almost comforting.

For an infinitesimal second, his arms tighten around me before relaxing again.

I never would have imagined him as affectionate, but he manages to pull it off without any awkwardness.

"But it would have," I say. "If you hadn't gotten there in time."

"Maybe not." He doesn't sound convinced.

"Probably. Cameron's not a good person." I chuckle as I say it, like it's a big joke, but it's the worst joke in the universe.

He tenses against me. "Why do you say that?"

I hesitate. I can't talk about it.

I remember, suddenly, that I shouldn't be able to do this. I shouldn't be able to sit in some guy's lap without freaking out. Although, I was already freaking out when he pulled me onto him, so maybe that's why I'm not wanting to scream and run or flinch and flail.

The fact that I'm okay with being held by him makes me feel uncomfortable. I untangle myself from him as coolly as possible—which means not cool at all—and sit on the couch far enough away so that we are no longer touching. "He's just...you know..." *A rapist.* The word whispers in my mind, and I try to shake it away. "A misogynistic asswipe. He cheated on me, pretended like he really liked me just to get into my pants." I shrug. "The usual thing."

Dean shakes his head. "What happened to Miss 'I'm an open book'?"

"What do you mean?"

"You're hiding something," he says.

"*I'm* hiding something? This is really coming from you, Mr. Secret McBrooding Pants?"

This makes him laugh. His head tilts back and the sound is deep and masculine. I like seeing him laugh—he doesn't do it nearly enough. My eyes are drawn to his strong neck, and I feel a sudden urge to bite it, followed by the urge to smack myself in the face. *Stop thinking about him that way*. I push the thought away.

"McBrooding pants," he repeats and then rolls his eyes. "You're ridiculous," he says.

"Yep," I agree.

We're silent for a moment. I examine my surroundings, but other than the high-tech set up in the entryway, there's not much to look at. I turn my head towards Dean only to find him staring back at me.

"Why are you set up like you're running from the mob?"

He groans. "Not the mob thing again." He shrugs. "It's just a security precaution. I deal with a lot of people's money and someone tried to rob me once. I got a good deal on a couple of security cameras from a friend. There's one inside and one outside and the footage is sent wirelessly to my laptop. Better safe than sorry."

"Oh." Tried to rob him? I feel like there's a story there, but I'm not sure I want to know.

"Are you hungry? Want to go get some lunch?" he asks.

I think I love you.

"Yes," I say. "That sounds perfect."

11

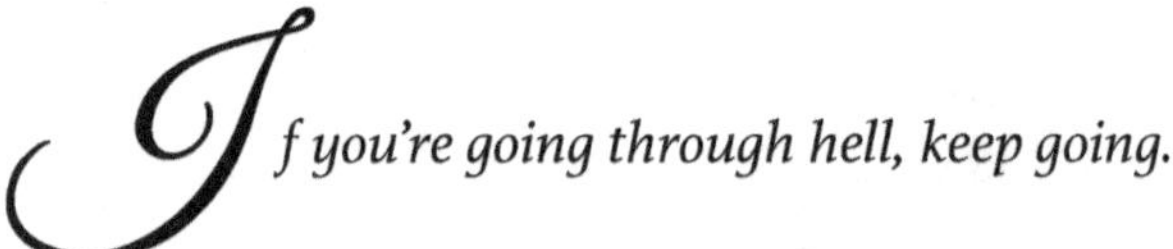

f you're going through hell, keep going.

—Winston Churchill

Dean

I take Freya to a little hole-in-the wall pizza parlor. She practically swoons when we enter the building. The smell of yeast, basil and garlic permeates the air.

"It smells amazing in here," she breathes.

She definitely needs some hangover food.

I sit her down at a booth and go and put in our order.

All I can think about while I wait in line is that I really need to kick the shit out of Cameron. I wish I would have done it last night, but it's better I didn't. I don't need to attract any kind of attention to myself, let alone anything of a violent nature. Not that I'm normally a violent person, because despite evidence to the contrary, I'm not.

But when I saw him, pulling her off into the darkness... and when she told me he might have drugged her...I could have lost my mind.

The place is packed and it takes a while to get the food. I know Freya must be hungry because when I get back to where she's sitting, her foot is jiggling up and down and she's not saying anything.

I place the little triangular card with our order number on the edge of the table and take the silent time to watch her while she watches for the food.

Her normally straight hair is still a little damp, and seems to be drying into loose waves. She looks good like this, natural, no makeup. Even with the gray smudges under her eyes, she's...pretty.

Who am I kidding? I always find her attractive, no matter how much she pisses me off. Last night she was pretty, too. Even when she was hammered, but before she started puking.

This morning, when I opened the door and she was practically naked...I only caught a glimpse, but from what I could tell, she's like a tiny little sprite of perfection. Perfect breasts, perfect narrow waist that flares into hips I would like to grab and then—

I look away from her, not really liking where my thoughts are going. I don't have time for a relationship, or anything even close to it and I doubt she returns the sentiment, anyway.

I wait until the food arrives and she's eaten a full slice before I ask what I've been thinking about all morning. Well, except for the thoughts of her general attractiveness which I have been trying to avoid.

"So, did you find anything out the other day? Any success with the girlfriends?"

We haven't spoken since we agreed to interrogate people close to the victims to try and find a connection other than me.

"Not really," she says. She tells me what they both said, which amounts to almost nothing, and she has me check the time I texted Daisy the night of the murder.

"Do you think that's important?" I ask, after checking my cell and confirming her story.

"I don't know," she says. "All I know is I don't really trust Daisy. I mean, I know hippies are all free love and everything, but she seems shady. What about you? Come up with any good leads?"

I shake my head at her and finish chewing the last bit of my pizza before chucking the crust on the plate.

"No luck," I say. "I couldn't get anyone to talk to me."

"Amazing," she teases, "since you're so approachable and unassuming."

I roll my eyes at her, even though I want to laugh. She's one of the only people who feels comfortable enough to tease me. Probably because most people find me a little intimidating. Now that I think of it, she's never seemed frightened of me, at all.

"An eye roll," she says. "That's better than a glare. I call that progress."

I glare at her, but she just grins at me around a mouth full of pizza, so I don't think it had the desired effect.

"Matt has a twin sister, but I can't seem to find her anywhere," I say. "Do you know Elizabeth Ellison?"

She freezes, a slice of pizza halfway to her mouth.

"Liz? Liz Ellison?" She drops the pizza. "Matt's twin sister is Liz the slut?"

"I'll take that as a yes?"

"Uh, yeah, I know her. She's the one that I caught sleeping with Cameron the douche." She blinks. "I saw her with her brother a few days before he was killed. The same day I hit you with my car."

She tells me about how she was in the bathroom and Liz apologized to her after her date.

I resist the urge to ask about this date. I also resist the tug of jealousy that pulls at my chest. It doesn't matter and it's none of my business.

She also tells me how Liz had black eyes and seemed upset when she was leaving with her brother.

"You don't think it was an accident—you think someone was beating her up? Maybe it was Curtis?"

Now it's her turn to roll her eyes at me and my inability to say Cameron's name.

"I don't know. She didn't say, and I got the impression they were over. I'm not sure it's relevant to your case. But, maybe I can get her to meet up and see if she knows if her brother had any enemies." She winces. "I really don't want to see her again—oh my God!" She sticks her hand out and it covers mine on the table.

I look down at her hand covering mine. I think this is the first time she's willingly touched me.

"I almost forgot. I saw her last night, too." She removes her hand from mine and then tells me how Liz came over to her table, but then took off immediately after Cameron arrived.

I nod and listen and we eat in silence for a few minutes. I ponder all of the information we have. It's not enough.

"Are you going to finish that?" she asks, pointing at the crust on my plate.

"Help yourself." I lift my hands so she can snatch it off my plate.

"Now what do we do?" she asks me, dipping the crust in ranch and sticking it in her mouth, but not before some of the sauce has fallen on her shirt.

"I don't know." I can't help but stare at the spot on her chest. She's a mess, but it's so cute.

"Do you have any enemies?"

"No."

"You have something..." I motion to my shirt in the same spot she's got a dollop of ranch.

"Oh." She looks down and grabs a napkin, wiping at it ineffectually, making the white stain spread instead of disappear.

I try not to laugh.

"No enemies?" she continues our conversation, throwing the dirty napkin down on her plate. "Maybe someone in your gambling circle who's lost a lot of money to you?"

"Well, yeah, a lot of people have lost a lot of money to

me. Are you suggesting one of them might be framing me for murder?"

She shrugs. "Maybe."

I shake my head. "I don't think so. What would be in it for them, other than revenge? They wouldn't get their money back, and they would run the risk of being charged with murder. Plus they would have to be totally nuts. I try not to let crazy people into the games."

"That's true, but how do you know if someone is over the deep end?"

"I guess I don't."

"Can you give me all your gambling records? I can give it to Lucy to go through and she can probably do something fancy with it, like cross-reference it with medical histories and criminal records."

"I'm not giving you all my information to pass over to someone I've never even met."

"Geez, defensive much? Lucy is absolutely trustworthy."

"I don't know that. I have a lot of people's private information encrypted into files that even I can't access. I'm not comfortable giving it to anyone."

"Okay, fine."

We eat in silence for a minute and then I ask, "Any other ideas?"

She chews up her food and swallows before asking, "Have any other chicks asked for your services?"

The table next to us, stuffed with tween girls and a disgruntled-looking dad, glances over at us.

“No.” I give her a dirty look and she just smiles innocently.

“As a matter of fact,” I tell her, “all of my businesses are starting to suffer. Word is getting around about all of this. My biggest gamblers have pulled out of the last two games. One of them is your buddy Caleb.”

That stops her. “Cameron?”

“Yep. Asswipe himself. I’m going to miss taking his money. You can add him to your list of people who’ve lost a lot to me, by the way.”

“He’ll be back,” she says, with a shake of her head. “He doesn’t have a lot of self-control.”

That gets my attention. “What’s that supposed to mean?”

“Nothing, nothing.” She waves a hand at me. “So, are you going to be okay, missing out on all that cash?”

I don’t know why she’s interested in my finances, but it bothers me more than it probably should.

“I have savings,” I say quickly. “The real question here is what we’re going to do next.”

“Well, we don’t have many options. Lucy’s still trying to get information from the police files. Other than that, we’ll have to wait it out, for now. Either someone else will end up dead, and you’ll be cleared since you won’t be involved, or no one ends up dead and the rumors die down and you’ll be back in business. Either way, if you get a call from any chicks asking to beat up their exes, let me know.”

“Why? What are you going to do?”

“*We*,” she points at me and then herself, “will stake it out.”

Stake it out?

"You know," she continues at my perplexed expression. "Wait around after you do the deed, and follow your victim to see if anyone else shows up to take it to the next level."

"That's a good idea," I say slowly, "but I don't think you should come with me."

"What do you mean? Why not?"

I shake my head. "Too dangerous."

"Look, buddy." She points a finger at me. "I'm either in or I'm out. Besides, I'll just be there to observe. You'll need a witness if the shit hits the fan. I promise to be on my best behavior and stay completely out of your way."

I don't like it, but she's right. "Fine."

She grins at me. I don't know what it is about her smiles, they're like everything else she does. She's fully invested in the expression and it fills her face and shines on everything around her.

"You're such a pushover," she says.

I try to hold it back, but I can't control it. It pushes at the top of my throat and I laugh out loud.

12

I know, my dear Watson, that you share my love of all that is bizarre and outside the conventions and humdrum routine of daily life.

—Arthur Conan Doyle

Freya

A week passes. Dean doesn't receive any calls, and we don't come up with any more leads. I put Lucy to task, but the firewall into the police computer records is locked tighter than a jar of pickles when you have lotion on your hands. She's still working on it, though.

I can tell Dean's getting antsy when I talk to him on the phone.

I spend most of the week recovering from the weekend and absorbed in classes. Spring break is rapidly approaching and I think my professors are trying to make up for the brain cells that will be lost with binge drinking by cramming as much work as possible into the next two weeks.

Bethany comes over one night. She brings me a bunch of my favorite foods and spends most of the night groveling about the night of the roofie incident. She thought I had gone home when she came back to the table and I was gone.

I assure her that it's fine, there was no way for her to know with her phone dead and all, but apparently Lucy read her the riot act.

"She was all calm and monotone." Bethany shakes her head. "It was the creepiest lecture I've ever received. Then she started asking all these questions about my family and upbringing and past. It was like she was trying to get into my brain!"

"She's a psychotherapist."

Bethany shrugs. "I know, but I'm not ready to be fixed yet."

On Thursday, I get the call from Dean. He's finally been approached by a vengeful ex.

"This one's really angry. She said she hopes I am a killer. She asked me to cut out his eyeballs and shove them in interesting places."

"That's adorable."

"Right? They broke up last week and he's got another girlfriend already, and she lives in Lincoln Hall."

Lincoln Hall is one of the fancier dorm buildings with private rooms and giant communal kitchens.

"Another girlfriend already, or someone he'd been seeing on the side?" I ask.

"I don't really care. My client seems to believe that he'll be exiting the building tonight at lights out. You ready?"

"As a virgin on prom night."

There's a pause and then he asks, "What does that mean? Does that mean you're nervous or excited?"

"I'm not sure exactly. Sometimes things just come out."

"I've noticed."

We plan to meet at my place at nine to get ready and set up since lights out is at ten.

When he gets to my place, I'm already dressed in all black from head to toe.

He walks in and raises an eyebrow at my outfit. "Why do you look like a football player?"

Maybe the black grease under my eyes is a bit over the top.

"So, you know, people can't see my face as much and stuff."

"Athletes use the black stripes under their eyes to avoid glare from the stadium lights, so they can see the ball easier."

"Oh." I was not aware of that. "Well, it looks cool, right?" I grin and blink my eyes up at him.

He shakes his head with a chuckle. "Are you ready to go?"

"Yep!" I'm really way too excited about this whole espionage thing.

We get in his car and he pulls out of my parking lot and heads towards campus.

"Did you bring walkie-talkies?" I ask.

"Why would I bring walkie-talkies?"

"Uh, duh, because they're fun."

"We don't need them, and you aren't going to be out of my sight for any longer than it takes for me to do the deed."

"Hmph."

He's a very conscientious driver. We pull up at a four-way stop and he allows the other driver to go, even though we got there first, before carefully pulling into the intersection.

His hands haven't left the 10-and-2 positions on the steering wheel since we got in the car.

"You drive like my grandmother," I observe.

"What?" He twists his head in my direction, a bewildered expression on his face, and then quickly looks back at the road. "I do not."

"Yes, you do."

"Well, you drive like a blind speed freak."

"No I don't!"

I do. I totally do.

"I'm just, you know, aggressive," I say.

He snorts. "Suicidal."

We're silent for a moment, the only sound is the tires humming against the pavement.

"Slowpoke," I say in low voice out of the corner of my mouth.

"Crazy person," he returns so quickly I wonder if he had the insult waiting.

"Snail," I say, louder.

"Weirdo."

I watch him, waiting for his rejoinder.

His gaze is still fixed firmly in front of him, but then he glances over and we both laugh.

It's one of those things that's not that funny, but for some reason it is. By the time we reach the lot at the far end of campus, we've managed to pull ourselves together. After he parks, he pulls out a picture of our victim, printed in color on an eight by ten piece of paper and hands it to me.

Our fingers brush and instead of freaking me out, a zing of electricity runs up my arm and down my chest, making butterflies take flight in my stomach.

That's not normal.

"This is the guy we're looking for. Tommy Boone," he says.

I ignore the zings and focus on the picture. It's a guy playing beer pong. He's fairly average-looking, skinny with dark hair and a hoodie. I hand the picture back to him and look around the desolate lot.

"Why are we parking all the way over here?" I ask.

"We're trying to be inconspicuous. It would probably be a bad idea to roll up in my very identifiable vehicle anywhere near where we plan on being."

"But now we have to walk forever. In the dark."

"You can stay in the car if you want," he says with a smirk. He grabs a small bag out of the backseat before pushing his door open and climbing out.

I clamber out of the car after him and walk quickly to catch up with him.

He's got long legs, and I practically have to run to keep up. When I nearly trip over my own feet, he grabs my hand.

"Be careful!" he whispers. I'm sure he's glaring at me, but it's too dark to make out his expression. We move hand in hand through a silent and dark campus, then through the quad, keeping to the edges, and wherever it's darkest.

His large hand is gripping mine in a warm grasp and the zings are flying all over the place. I'm not freaking out from the contact like I normally would, and I feel like freaking out because I'm not freaking out.

Shit. My palms are getting sweaty. How gross. Should I pull away? Would it be weird if I did?

I don't want him to think that I'm thinking too much about it, because then it would get weird. Screw it, I'm already weird.

We finally stop outside the dorms, behind a hedge of bushes that are just starting to get their spring bloom. He releases my hand.

"Now what?" I ask him in a whisper.

"Now we wait for Tommy to leave. When he does, we'll follow. The ex told me he lives in Granger, so he'll be walking back. You'll have to stay out of sight while I do the deed. Then we'll follow him," he whispers back.

We're silent for a moment.

"Are you really going to shove his balls up his ass or whatever?" I ask.

"What kind of question is that?" He sounds offended. "Of course not."

"Then what are you going to do?"

He opens the small bag he brought with him from the

car and pulls out a clown mask. He holds it up a little so I can see it in the light shining from the nearby dorm building. It's one of those big rubber faces that you pull over your head. It's got white skin, giant red lips, red nose and curly rainbow hair.

"That's fucking creepy," I say.

"Right?" He sounds way too excited.

"You like that thing," I accuse.

He shrugs. "I love this kind of stuff. No violence, pure entertainment. You'll see."

"You're not going to hurt him?"

"I'm not even going to touch him."

A few minutes later, the doors open and a small group of people exits, talking and laughing. We have to wait and watch a few more stragglers leave before our target emerges.

I recognize Tommy from the photo, although his hair is a bit longer now and it's mussed like he and his new girlfriend have been doing something naughty, naughty.

He heads down the sidewalk path, whistling, and moving past our hiding spot, blissfully unaware of our presence or malicious intentions.

"Let's go this way," Dean whispers.

He grabs my hand again and we head quickly in the opposite direction, rounding the next building by moving through the trees and grass to cut our victim off where his path will turn to take him to his dorm building.

We reach the corner of a large brick building and Dean stops. "Stay here." He squeezes my hand slightly, hands me the empty bag that previously held the mask, and then he runs over to where the sidewalk path makes a sharp turn. I peek around the corner of the wall and watch while he stops directly underneath an arching street light.

I can hear Tommy, still whistling as his path moves to intercept where Dean is.

Peeking around the corner of the building at Dean, I shake my head in amazement. It's the perfect spot, really. Tommy won't see him until he rounds the corner about fifteen feet away, and when he does, he's going to shit his pants. Dean is standing eerily still in the dome of the light, staring in the direction Tommy is approaching. He's wearing the clown mask, and this total Freddie Krueger outfit—black pants and a blue and red striped shirt.

Suddenly, the whistling stops. From my vantage point, I have a clear view of Dean, but I would have to move into view to get a good shot of Tommy.

"Holy shit," I hear Tommy murmur.

Dean still doesn't move.

The silence extends, and then Dean clenches his fists and cocks his head.

The movement is subtle, but he was so motionless before that he might as well leap around snapping and snarling.

I hear a shuffling movement from Tommy's direction, followed by a thud. If I had to guess, I would say he just fell on his ass.

Dean's clown face turns in my direction and then he shrugs. He pulls his phone out of his pocket and takes a picture in Tommy's direction.

I creep out a little further to see what's going on. Tommy is passed out on the ground.

Dean creeps closer to him and stares for a long moment before taking another picture and walking quickly and quietly away, back towards me, pulling the mask off his head.

"That was easier than I expected," he whispers, once he's leaning next to me against the wall.

"Is he okay?" I ask in a low voice.

He takes the bag that I'm still holding and shoves the mask back inside of it. "He's good, just fainted. And pissed his pants. I sent the picture to my client to use as she pleases."

"Vengeful."

"It is the business you started."

"I guess."

He's craning around the corner of the building to keep an eye on Tommy, and at my words, he turns his head back around.

"What?" He looks at me and I can tell he's trying to see my eyes, but it's fairly dark in the shadow of the building. "You regret making me beat up Christian?"

"Cameron," I correct. "And no. I don't regret it. It was gratifying at the time, but..."

"But what?"

I shrug. "I've changed. If I knew then what I know now, I wouldn't have done it."

"Why?"

"Revenge is fleeting. Moving on with your life is forever."

"Wise words from the girl who impersonated a lawyer on behalf of some guy she hardly knows."

I chuckle at that. "Yep, I'm a regular philosopher."

"Why are you helping me?" he asks suddenly. "You were dead set against it, and then you changed your mind. What changed it?"

"Well, in addition to philosophizing, I'm a real bleeding heart," I say. "Feeder of starving children, helper of the homeless, fighter of the man." I'm really getting into this now. "Supporter of the underdog, savior of the weak."

"I'm hardly weak," he scoffs. "And I'm serious. Why are you helping me?"

I really don't want to tell him I'm using him as a means to get over personal trauma, but I'm not really sure what else to say. I already tried the bleeding heart bit.

A moan emanates from Tommy's general vicinity, interrupting our conversation, and Dean curses under his breath.

Saved by the victim. Nice.

Dean peeps around the corner, and I have no clue what's going on.

"He's getting up," Dean whispers to me after a moment.

I watch Tommy stumble into our line of vision. His back is to us, as he walks down the sidewalk to his dorm, head whipping all around, probably searching for the psycho clown killer that was there moments ago.

His footsteps quicken and Dean grabs my hand again. "Come on," he says, "don't want to lose sight of him."

We follow at a discreet distance, ducking around bushes and buildings until we're just outside Granger Hall.

Dean stops us behind a tree. He has my back against the trunk, and he's facing me, his hands resting on my shoulders. He peers occasionally around me to watch Tommy go inside.

He's touching me, and I'm not freaking out.

He's standing so close, my nose brushes his shirt and he smells *amazing*, like citrus and cinnamon, and for a brief glorious moment I want to lean into his muscular chest, and wrap my arms around him. Then maybe he'd pick me up and I would wrap my legs around his waist, and he would stick his tongue—

"Freya," he says, jarring me from my fantasy.

"Dean," I say, a bit too breathlessly.

"He's inside now," he says.

"Okay."

"I guess we should stay here and wait a little bit? What do you think?"

"That sounds good." I'm gazing up at him, only half listening. I can barely make out his face in the dark. There's a few street lamps nearby, but they are all behind him, casting his face in shadow.

"He's probably going to be okay," Dean whispers.

I really wish he would whisper something a little sexier.

"I mean, you need a key to get into the dorm," he continues. "And they've got cameras and stuff."

That's...not really what I had in mind.

"Right," I whisper back.

He doesn't seem to notice the lusty turmoil raging inside of me.

He sighs and peeks around the tree again. His hands are still on my shoulders and he moves them down my arms, rubbing gently up and down, like he doesn't realize he's doing it.

But then his face tilts down towards mine. "You're arms are really soft."

He stops rubbing them, but his hands are still cupping my upper arms gently.

"I make a salt scrub," I say.

"What?"

"Yeah, with kosher salt and coconut oil." Stupid. Why am I telling him this? He doesn't care!

"Oh."

He's still looking down at me and I'm still looking up at him, and he starts to lean forward, his mouth approaching mine, and all I can think is, *yes*, but then we're interrupted.

By my cell phone.

The ringtone is Kristina Debarge's "Goodbye," specially input under Cameron's number, and the music is emanating from the vicinity of my bosom. I forgot I stuffed my phone in my bra when I was getting dressed.

Oops.

I pull it out and silence it, right after making a face at Cameron's name. Gross. I stick it back down my shirt.

At some point, Dean removed his hands from me, and now his arms are crossed over his chest and I think I'm getting the ultra-death glare, level ten. I can't see it, but I can feel it.

"You brought your cell phone?" he whispers angrily.

"I forgot I—"

"And you didn't even think to put it on silent? We're lucky it didn't go off before, you could have compromised this whole thing!"

"Listen, I'm sorry, I—"

"Sorry? You're *sorry*?"

Okay. He is way too pissed off over one tiny little mistake.

"You know what? Fuck you!" I'm trying to whisper, but it's difficult when I'm angry. I push against his chest, an exercise in futility, but he steps back far enough for me to stomp away from him.

"Freya, wait," he says from behind me.

"Go suck a toaster."

I don't care anymore if someone sees me. I take the brightly lit sidewalk and march down it like a woman on a mission. And I am on a mission, a mission to get away from Mr. Hottie McGrumpy Pants.

He easily catches up to me and stops me with a hand on my arm.

I spin around, ready to read him the riot act. I open my mouth, but before any words come out, he's kissing me.

It's awkward at first. You really shouldn't begin a kiss—especially a first kiss—with your mouth open. It should start with your mouth closed and then progress from there.

Not this one. Somehow, the situation rectifies itself, but it takes a few long seconds of me figuring out what's happening to my mouth, while he nibbles at my lips and my anger fluctuates into something else entirely.

He's kissing me. Dean is kissing me. The most remarkable part is that I'm not flinching. I don't want to run away.

Exactly the opposite, actually. I want to get closer to him. I want him to surround me, I want him over me. I want him everywhere.

Dean is like the vaccine to the Cameron virus.

I think he feels the same way, if his actions are any indication. His lips are hungry and firm, yet somehow soft all at once and the way he's holding me against him makes me feel fragile and desired. Not at all like when Cameron kissed me, like he was trying to spell the alphabet with his tongue or something.

My hands are gripping his shoulders, holding myself upright to avoid dissolving into a puddle at his feet. His fingers trail along the line between my shirt and pants, and when he slips his hands under my shirt to span my waist, I can't help but arch against him and moan into his mouth.

"Holy hell," he says. His hands flex against my skin, and he presses me away, fingers still on my waist.

I feel a bit dazed as I look at him and try to catch his expression. He looks just as out of it as I feel, and his lips are swollen.

"I..." he says.

In the light of the moon and lamps littered along the sidewalk, I can see the confusion and uncertainty in his eyes.

"We should go," I say after a moment, putting him out of his misery.

He nods.

We walk back to his car in silence. I'm not sure what to say. I'm not sure what any of it means, if anything.

We get into the car, he still opens my door for me, but

then the drive home is shrouded in...nothing. Absolute silence, except for the hum of the tires against the road, and the occasional tick of the blinker when Dean has to make a turn.

I'm not sure what to think about what just happened. Should I think about it? Did it mean anything? My thought is no. I mean, maybe he was just trying to shut me up so I would still help him. I know he's not interested in me that way, he can't possibly like me. He doesn't act like it. And while it's intriguing to me that I didn't flinch away, like I've done with every other guy since Cameron, I know it would be a bad idea to pursue anything with him. He doesn't exactly fit the criteria that I need. I'm done with jerks. Been there, done that, got the souvenir that says "I dated the world's biggest douche and all I got was this T-shirt," and I can't go back there.

I made a promise to myself after Cameron that I would have more self-respect. I wouldn't be *that* girl, the one who goes for the guy that treats her like crap. No matter how hot he is and how much he resembles Thor. Although...Cameron was incredibly charming and sweet to begin with and turned into a jerk. Dean has never pretended to not be a jerk. He's been the same way the whole time.

Either way, I can't risk it.

I glance over at Dean while he's driving. It's too dark to make out his expression. He's staring out the windshield, eyes on the road, of course. I wonder what he's thinking. Is he thinking to himself, *smooth move, keeping the girl involved because I need her*. Or maybe he's thinking, *wow Freya is an awesome kisser and I really want to bang her.* Probably a combination of the two.

He must feel my gaze on him, because he glances over at me and I quickly avert my eyes.

Doesn't matter. No banging will be happening here. I cannot let myself get involved, I cannot lose my heart again to someone who doesn't love me back. And unfortunately, sex tends to lead to emotions. Dammit. Why can't I be like a dude?

I was twenty-one when I lost my virginity—way later than everyone I've ever known. Most of my friends lost theirs in high school. I was...a late bloomer. Seriously. I mean, I dated guys, but I never really felt that spark or attraction, at least not enough to let them stick their penis in me. Not until Cameron. And I am so scared that I will never find it again. I mean, if it took me twenty-one years to find it the first time, will I have to wait another twenty-one to feel it again?

But now there's Dean.

I'm definitely attracted to him. But what if I make the same mistake? Isn't that the definition of insanity, trying the same thing over and over and expecting different results?

He drops me off after an abrupt "Good night" and "I'll call you." I trudge up the stairs to my apartment, all the while trying to push him from my mind.

As I'm unlocking my door, my phone starts ringing again, this time the ring tone is "The Calculation" by Regina Spektor.

Lucy.

I open my door and then pull my phone out of my bra. "Hey Luce, what's crack-a-lackin'?"

"I was able to get into a portion of the police files and obtain some information."

Good ol' Lucy, right to the point. I lock my door behind me and flick on the lights. "Anything good?"

"A few things. The coroner calculated the time of death for both victims at approximately 11:00 p.m. They were able to confirm that the same weapon was used in both homicides. Also, Daisy McHenry made two statements. One when Jesse was murdered, detailing her whereabouts and alibi for the night. But, the way it's written isn't good for Dean. She describes him as a sociopath, and it's very incriminating. The second statement she submitted after Matt's death. She's the one that informed the police that he was the connection."

I throw myself onto the couch. "Hippie beyotch. Peace and love my ass!"

"I find it interesting that she seems determined to implicate Dean. It makes me suspicious. I think we should investigate her alibi a little more closely than the cops may have."

"Sounds fun. When?"

"Her friend who verified her alibi is out of town at a basketball game. We'll have to question her when she returns, which will be Thursday. We can go to her place of residence after your last class."

"I'm in. I'll pick you up."

We hang up and I lie on the couch for a few minutes,

thinking. I'm glad Lucy called, but it means I'll have to call Dean and let him know.

I think about his mouth on mine, the way he held me and the way my body responded like a firecracker. Then, I think about him stepping away and not speaking the entire way home.

I really don't want to talk to him right now.

I really don't want to think about him right now.

Maybe I'll call him tomorrow.

Maybe.

13

I think that if you live long enough, you realize that so much of what happens in life is out of your control, but how you respond to it is in your control.

—Hillary Clinton

Dean

Most people think the worst thing about hospitals is the food. That's not true. The worst part about hospitals is they tell their patients to sleep, and then they wake them up every hour to monitor their vitals.

It's two o'clock in the morning, and I'm trying to finish a paper that's due tomorrow without waking up my mom. She caught some kind of flu and became so dehydrated, I had to take her to the hospital. They wanted to keep her for observation and now we've been here for two days.

Sarah's staying with our neighbor. I've been running ragged between the hospital, school, making sure the fights are lined up, and making sure Sarah has everything she needs.

The only bonus is that I've been at the hospital so much, I'm on a first-name basis with most of the nurses and they let me stay when they probably shouldn't.

I stare at the glowing screen of my laptop in the darkened hospital room and watch the cursor beat in time to my heart.

I should be thinking about my paper. Or my mom. Or my sister. Or the fact that I could very likely be charged with murder at any given moment. Instead, I'm thinking about one of the most infuriating women I've ever met. Who also happens to be the silliest, most kissable woman I've ever met.

I'm an asshole.

I didn't mean to kiss her.

I can't say I'm sorry I did.

She probably wanted to talk about it or something, after. I know how girls are with these things—I have a mother and a sister. I do feel sorry that I said nothing. But what could I say? I can't promise her anything. I have nothing to give her. I have nothing to offer. It's not like she likes me. She thinks I'm an ass. I have been an ass. And after she dated that piece of crap Carmichael, she deserves someone who can give her everything.

Or something, anything, which is more than I have. I

have no time for relationships. I don't even have time to sleep. I also don't have time to dwell. I have work to do.

I tap out a few sentences and pause when Mom shifts on the bed and mumbles something in her sleep. After a moment of watching her until she seems to be sleeping peacefully again, I turn back towards my computer. Instead of seeing the words on the screen, I see Freya's face the moment after I kissed her. Eyes dazed, lips swollen. That damn black shit under her eyes.

The thought makes me want to laugh out loud, but I stifle it into a grin that spreads across my face.

"What are you looking at that's giving you such a goofy smile?" my mom says.

My head jerks in her direction. I didn't realize she was awake.

"Nothing," I say quickly, schooling my expression into seriousness. "Sorry if I woke you. I was just working on a term paper."

"You didn't wake me. I think my body is in tune to the next time I can expect to be woken by a diligent nurse." She offers me a sleepy smile. "You should go home, you'll probably get more done," she says.

"It's okay. I don't want to leave in case you need something."

"I don't need anything, Dean. You don't need to sacrifice your life all the time. I'll be fine."

The nurse walks in then—a dark-skinned woman with sleek black hair tied back and soft pink scrubs. She clicks on the bedside lamp and exchanges quiet pleasantries with

Mom while she takes Mom's temperature and blood pressure.

"As long as everything is still good, the doctor should release you tomorrow," the nurse tells my mom while she wraps up the cords and puts them on her little trolley.

"Oh, good," Mom says. "As much as I love your company, I can't wait to go home."

"Well, as much as we love having you, I don't want to see you again anytime soon."

They laugh softly—hospital humor—and the nurse leaves on quiet feet, the only sound is the squeak of the wheels as she pulls the blood pressure machine out with her.

Once she's gone, Mom looks at me. "Are you going to tell me what you were smiling about, before?"

"No."

"Is it a girl? Because I'm pretty sure term papers don't make people smile like that."

I hesitate. I don't want to lie to her, but my reluctance to answer gives me away.

"It is a girl!" She smiles at me, looking entirely too excited at the prospect. "What's her name?"

"Mom, I don't have time for girls."

"Just because you don't have time, doesn't mean it's not going to happen. Do you love her?"

"What? No!"

She makes a face. "Is she mean, like Angelica?"

"No."

"Based on that smile earlier, I didn't think so."

"Can we not talk about this?"

"What would you rather talk about?"

"Anything? How are you feeling?"

"Ugh." She waves her hand at me. "I do not want to talk about me or my health. We need to talk about you, Dean. You deserve more happiness, and less chaos and work."

"Deserving something doesn't entitle you to it."

She watches me for a few long seconds. "You're right. It doesn't. But if you *don't* consider yourself once in a while—your needs, and what makes you happy—you're going to burn out and crash. And then you'll be no good to anyone."

I turn away from her caring face and stare back at my computer screen that needs at least 2,000 more words on it before I can let myself relax.

"I have regrets, Dean," she says after a moment of silence. "My life is full of them."

I look over and I can see her eyes shining in the dim light.

"You only get one turn on this planet. What's the point, if you're not living it?"

I want to argue with her. I want to tell her I *am* living it. That she and Sarah *are* my life and I have no point without them. But I can't lie.

"Maybe you're right," I finally say.

"I'm your mother. I'm always right."

14

The pursuit of truth will set you free; even if you never catch up with it.

–Clarence Darrow

Freya

"And then he kissed me," I tell Lucy.

"How was it?" she asks.

I pause for a second, trying to come up with the best way to describe it. "Amazing," I finally settle on, but then have to add, "Mind-numbingly amazing."

"Good. Now keep your eyes on the road."

I do as told and squint at the street signs. "Where did you say this place was?"

"It's not far. You're going to turn right after this next street."

"But then," I continue, "he pushed me away."

We're heading to some student housing, a few blocks away from campus. Daisy's statement said that she had spent the night at her friend Natalie's house. Natalie lives with three other people. All four residents verified that Daisy had been there all night.

"He pushed you away?" She raises her eyebrows at me.

I turn where Lucy told me, and we pull into the parking lot. The student housing looks like regular apartments, but I had been to parties here before and each house has four bedrooms for four residents, and they share a living space, kitchen and two bathrooms.

I park in front of the building where Daisy was (allegedly) the night of Jesse's murder and turn towards Lucy.

"Not like that," I assure her. "He was gentle. He didn't really push me, he sort of set me away from him."

"And then what?"

"And then he took me home. That was it."

"Did you discuss what happened between you?"

"No." I shake my head. "He didn't say anything the whole way home."

"You didn't say anything either?" She wrinkles her nose at me. "I find that difficult to believe."

"Hardy har har." I roll my eyes at her. "I didn't know what to say. When he dropped me off, he said he would call me later. That was five days ago, Lucy. Five days! I don't know why I'm tripping about it. It's not like I like him. He's a jerk."

"You haven't heard from him since?"

"Well," I concede. "He texted me the next day to let me know that Tommy was still alive. That was it. And I tried to call him back because I haven't been able to find Liz the slut and ask her about her brother. Then, I tried again yesterday to tell him about this lead." I gesture to the building in front of us. "I wanted to talk to him about that stuff at least, but he didn't answer."

"Did you leave a message?"

"No," I scoff. "I don't want to seem desperate. Or like, I'm into him or something. Because I'm not. I'm totally not. It means nothing that he's the only man I've met since Cameron who doesn't make me want to vomit my intestines all over his face."

"Well, I would—"

"Bully him into submission? I know," I interrupt. She totally would, too. You should have seen when she first decided she wanted to use Jensen to learn about romantic relationships. She seriously stalked the poor fool and harassed him until he caved. He had no idea who he was dealing with.

Of course, it actually worked for her.

"I was going to say," she gives me a pointed look, "that I would wait until he calls you again. You know he will. As a matter of fact, he was the one who contacted you in the first place to enlist your assistance, and it doesn't sound like he has anyone else." She pats me on the leg. "Just sit tight. It will all work itself out."

"There's nothing to work out. In fact, we shouldn't even be having this conversation. I don't know why I brought it up, because I don't care about Dean. He's an ass." And with that complete lie, I get out of the car and wait for Lucy to crawl out the driver's side before shutting it behind her.

We walk up to the door and knock. A few seconds later, it swings open to reveal a tall, gorgeous black girl in short-shorts and a tank top.

"Are you Natalie Winchester?" Lucy asks in her standard, formal tone.

"Who's asking?" the girl at the door asks, one hand on her hip.

"My name is Lucy London, and this is Freya Morgan. We want to ask a few questions about the night of Jesse Carmichael's death."

"Why?"

"Our friend is suspected of the murder, and we want to verify Daisy's version of events."

If it had been up to me, I would have come up with some cockamamie story about doing research for my thesis or something, but not Lucy. Right to the point and too damn honest. We'll be lucky if we aren't thrown out on our ear, and this Natalie Winchester doesn't look exactly friendly.

After a second of silence, the girl turns and walks inside, leaving the door open for us to follow. "Come on in," she calls out behind her.

Lucy and I look at each other.

I shrug and walk in. It looks like most college student

apartments: kinda messy, with empty beer bottles on the counter and a giant glass bong on the coffee table.

The girl—whom I'm assuming is Natalie—plops into an oversized chair. Lucy stands awkwardly in the entryway, and I sit on the edge of the couch.

"Ask away." She waves her hand at us.

"What time did Daisy arrive the night of the murder?" I ask.

"Around six."

"Can you give us a detailed description of the events that transpired from the time she arrived until the following morning?" Lucy asks.

She shrugs. "There's not much to tell. She came over. We had a bunch of people here. We drank some beer, smoked some weed...that part, we didn't tell the cops." She's quiet for a second and then snorts out a laugh. "Daisy got a little sick. I told her, 'You can't smoke after drinking. Pot after liquor, never been sicker,' but did she listen? Nope. She was puking in the bathroom for like an hour."

"That's not in her statement," Lucy says. No doubt she memorized the entire thing.

"No shit, probably because she didn't want to get busted for the weed."

"Approximately what time did Daisy get sick?" Lucy asks.

"I don't know." She stops and thinks for a minute. "It was right after Jason got home from work—he's one of my roommates—so it must have been like ten thirty or something."

Ten-thirty. That was just after Dean texted Daisy. Coincidence? I think not. But I have no idea what it means.

Lucy must be thinking something along the same lines, except in hyperdrive because she says, "Can we see the bathroom she used?"

I look over at her. Why the hell do we want to see the scene of the vomit?

Natalie seems as surprised at the question as I am.

"Sure."

We follow her down a narrow hallway to the small bathroom. "Here it is."

"Thanks," Lucy says. She hurries into the room. She is way too excited about this.

It looks like a normal bathroom to me. Tub, toilet, sink.

Lucy flings back the shower curtain. They seriously need some scrubbing bubbles in here. The tile is a disaster. There's a couple of bottles of shampoo and conditioner lying on the bottom of the tub.

There's also a small window—about four feet wide and two feet tall—above where the tile ends and the wall begins. The window is open to let in the air, no screen or anything.

"Thank you for all your help," Lucy says suddenly, and then she's stalking past me and out towards the door.

"Um. Yeah, thanks Natalie. Nice to meet you."

I hurry after Lucy.

"What the bananas is going on?" I ask her when we exit the apartment.

She doesn't stop to answer me. Instead of heading for my car, she walks around the side of the building.

"Daisy was in the bathroom for about an hour," she says.

I follow her down a narrow space between two buildings. There's not even enough room for us to walk side by side.

"Yeah, and?"

"And what if she wasn't in the bathroom the entire time?"

"What do you mean?"

She stops suddenly, making me halt in my tracks behind her. She turns towards the building and nods up at the open window. It's the bathroom window we were just looking at minutes ago.

"What if she received the text from Dean, faked being sick, went to the bathroom, climbed out the window and killed Jesse, then returned the same way?"

I look up at the window, the narrow space and the six foot drop. "Seems like a lot of work to kill some asshole."

"Over fifty percent of victims are killed by someone they know, and more than a third of that number involves romantic relationships."

"Okay, but we need more evidence. All this is circumstantial. And why would she kill Matt, too?"

"I don't know." Her face is pensive as she examines the window, and then her gaze moves around the building and down to the hard-packed dirt ground. "I was hoping we would find more clues or something," she says.

I glance around as well. "No trail of bloody footprints here, Scoob."

She sighs. "I can see that."

"How would she have gotten back into the bathroom? She's not much bigger than I am, and that window is pretty high up there."

"I'm not sure. I will have to do more research," she says resolutely, and then frowns. "But I'm not sure where to start."

"Ruh-roh!"

She rolls her eyes at me.

"Come on." I sling an arm around her shoulder. "Let's get back to the mystery van, and we'll figure something out over dinner."

"Do you want another egg roll?" Lucy asks.

I snort. "Is that a rhetorical question?"

We're sitting in front of the TV at my place, munching on Chinese takeout and watching *Pitch Perfect.*

I grab the last egg roll and dip it in sweet and sour sauce. Lucy's done eating anyway—she's pulled out her laptop and is tapping away, barely paying attention to me.

"Any luck getting more intel out of the police records?" I ask.

"No."

"What about security on campus? Do they have cameras anywhere?"

Her fingers hover over the keyboard and she looks up at me. "That's a good idea. I'll have to see if they have cameras and where they're located. It will be fairly easy to narrow down which footage to view since we have a more exact time of death for both murders."

"Will it be easy to hack into the system if they have one?"

"Most likely, but I'm not sure yet," she murmurs.

There's silence for a moment while I watch the movie and she types away.

"Did you check social media sites to see if there's a connection between Daisy and Matt?"

"Yes," she says, "and I could not find a viable association."

I blow my breath out of my mouth with a huff. "You know, as much as I want Daisy to be the killer, I just don't see how we can prove she killed her own boyfriend, let alone someone she apparently didn't know."

"Mmhmm."

She's totally into the computer and not listening to me at all, I can tell.

"Maybe the killer is a three-legged orangutan."

"Hmmm."

"Or a one-armed man. I've heard that's a popular theory."

She nods.

"I'm pregnant."

Nothing.

"It's yours."

"What?"

I sigh. "You're a freak, but I love you."

"Okay."

A couple hours later, Lucy leaves and I'm straightening up when there's a knock at the door.

"Did you forget something?" I call out as I walk to answer. She literally just left. But it's not like her to forget anything—her brain is like a steel trap.

I swing open the door and it's not Lucy on my doorstep.

It's Cameron.

"What are you doing here?"

"Can I come in?" He's standing there, hands in pockets, dressed in jeans and a T-shirt, smiling disarmingly.

My hands tighten on the door knob. "Um, I don't think so. It's late. I was just getting ready for bed."

"Were you?" he asks with a smirk.

My stomach knots. I should not have mentioned the word *bed* in his presence.

"Why are you here?" I ask again.

I haven't talked to him since the night at the bar when I vomited all over Dean. I'm still on the fence about whether Cameron actually roofied me or not. I mean, he's scum, but I can't imagine him doing something that nefarious. He's more like a child. A stupid, selfish child.

"I miss you," he says. "I just want to talk. Hang out." He shrugs. "Maybe get to know each other again." He sounds odd, jittery.

I laugh, but there's no humor in the sound. "That sounds like crazy talk. Goodbye, Cameron."

I move to shut the door, but he stops it with his hand.

My heart starts beating rapidly. What if he forces his way inside? What if...

"I know it was you," he says, his voice suddenly cold, his eyes dark.

"What?"

"Don't play stupid, Freya. Someone's spreading rumors that I have gonorrhea, and I know it was you."

Gonorrhea? I would laugh, if I wasn't so freaked out.

"I didn't spread any rumors," I say.

"I could come in right now and you wouldn't be able to stop me. I could do whatever I want to you. Remember, Freya?"

Shit.

"I remember—" I start and then in the middle of the sentence, I slam the door as hard and as quickly as I can, locking it with trembling fingers.

My body is covered in chills that won't quit. I knew Cameron was a fucked-up asshole, but I didn't realize how far his douchebaggery went. Why would he come here? Why would he do this?

I try to pull it together.

"What I remember is how insignificant your penis is," I call out. I wish I could think of a better comeback, but I'm too terrified to come up with a wittier response.

He laughs and then there's a loud bang, like he hit his fist on the door, making me jump. "Too scared to tell me that to my face, girlie?"

I race to the living room and grab my phone from where I left it on the couch. "I'm calling the cops!" I yell in the direction of the door. My hands are shaking too much for me to use my phone effectively. I walk around my apartment, making sure all my windows are locked and closed.

Even though I'm on the second floor, I just feel better checking.

I sit on my couch and stare down at my phone. I don't want to call the cops, even though I know I should. Without thinking too much about it, my fingers find Dean's number in my contact list and I hit the call button.

15

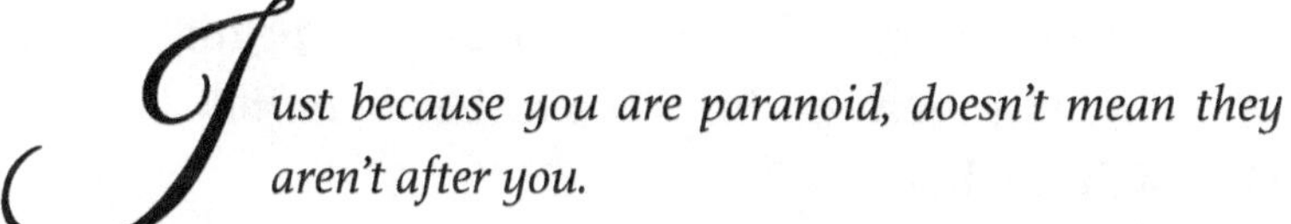

Just because you are paranoid, doesn't mean they aren't after you.

—Joseph Heller

Dean

I've just gotten back from taking Mom home from the hospital when my phone rings. I really hope it's not another disaster. I answer without looking at the number. "Hey."

"Dean." It's Freya. "Um, I, Cameron is here and I don't know—"

"What? Are you okay?" My heart has sputtered into

overdrive, and I'm already heading for the door, keys in hand.

"Yes, yes. I'm...I'm okay, I think. He just showed up and he wouldn't let me close the door."

"Where is he now?"

"Outside."

"And where are you?"

"Inside."

"Good. Don't move, I'll be right there."

I drive faster than I probably should, but it still feels like it takes forever to drive the mile to Freya's apartments. When I get there, I look around as I'm jogging to her building and then up the stairs to her door, but I see no sign of the asshole.

"Freya." I call, after knocking. "It's me, you can open up. I think he's gone."

The door swings open and she looks freaked the fuck out. I immediately step inside and wrap my arms around her small frame. I probably shouldn't do this, but the compulsion to comfort her, to make it all better, is inordinately strong. I need the comfort almost as much as she does.

"Are you okay?" I ask.

She nods against my chest. "I think so."

"I checked around your building, and I couldn't find him. What kind of car does he have?"

"A black Audi."

"Of course he does. Fucking douche." I reluctantly pull away and glance around her apartment. "Do you have any weapons or anything? I left in kind of a hurry and didn't grab anything from my place."

"Um." Her forehead creases as she thinks. "I have a baseball bat," she says finally, then she steps over to a closet near the entryway and pulls it out.

After she hands it to me, I head for the door. "I'll be right back. Lock the door behind me."

I wait on the other side of the door until I hear her engage the lock. I'm pretty sure Cameron has vacated the premises —I would have seen him on my way up, or he would have seen me—but it doesn't hurt to check. I walk around the dark building, and then check out the parking lot and down the street in either direction for his car, but he seems to be gone.

I head back to Freya's apartment and knock on the door again.

I hear her come to the door and stop for a second, probably looking at me through the peephole before opening the door.

She looks worse than before. She looked freaked when I first got there, and now she looks freaked and exhausted.

After letting me in, she turns and heads back into the living room. I lock the door behind us and follow her.

"He's gone," I tell her. "I checked everywhere. All the parking lots and down the street, couldn't find him."

"Good." She nods, her gaze on the floor.

"Are you okay?"

"I'm fine."

"You're shaking."

"Uh, I forgot to tell you, I'm a meth addict and I really

need a hit." She clenches her hands in her lap but it doesn't entirely stop the tremors.

"Do you always use humor to mask your emotions?"

"Is there something wrong with that?"

I'm sure she's in emotional overload and that's why she's acting moody. That's something I can relate to.

"We should call the cops," I say.

"No. Hell no," she responds immediately.

"Why not?"

"I don't want to talk to them about him."

"If there's a report against him, and then he does something bad to you or anyone else, there will be evidence and a history to back up the story. You can build a case against him."

"I can't, I just can't do that right now." She swallows and looks a bit ill. "Besides, what did he do, really? He came over, acted creepy and left. I'm not sure that's illegal. They'll think I'm overreacting, and I probably am."

"Okay, okay," I say, making my voice as calm as possible. "Maybe tomorrow we can go down and file a complaint or something."

"You really want to go back to jail?"

"I would do it for you."

I can't believe I just said that. It's true though. I'm starting to care for this girl more than I probably should. In order to avoid saying anything else I'll regret, I get up and head into the kitchen.

"What are you doing?" she asks.

"I'm hungry." I'm not, but she probably needs to eat.

"I don't have much food," she calls.

"I'll manage," I call back.

About ten minutes later, I make my way back into the living room with a plate of grilled cheese sandwiches and a large bowl of soup.

She hasn't moved from her same position on the couch, staring into space.

I need to get her to snap out of it.

"Here." I hand her a sandwich with a napkin and a spoon.

She eats and we share the bowl of soup. Once we're done, I take the dishes back to the kitchen.

When I've finished cleaning up, I go back into the living room. She still hasn't moved. I sit down next to her on the small couch, our knees touching.

"Are you going to tell me what happened?" I ask.

She tells me, in a halting voice, about how Lucy came over, she left and Cameron arrived. She tells me how he seemed strung out and accused her of spreading rumors he had gonorrhea.

"Gonorrhea?" I ask, raising my eyebrows at her.

"That wasn't me," she says. "I swear."

"It sounds like you," I say.

"It does," she agrees. "But I didn't."

"Would you be mad if I told you it was me?" I smile at her.

Her eyes widen and she smacks me in the arm. "You didn't!"

"I did. I didn't mean to, it just happened. I was so pissed after the whole incident the other weekend. That guy is such an asshole."

She gives a short laugh. "That also sounds like me."

I feel an immediate sense of relief when she laughs. It seems to relax her, get her out of the zone she's been in.

"Maybe you're rubbing off on me," I say, nudging her knee with mine.

"Can I rub myself on you?" she asks, and immediately slaps her hand over her mouth, her face flushing red. She turns away from me, grabbing a pillow off the couch and trying to hide in it.

I can't help but laugh, even though I'm trying not to because I don't want to embarrass her.

"Hey," I pat her back.

She sits up but won't meet my eyes, and her face is still red. "I…don't know where that came from, I'm sorry."

"Why are you apologizing?" I'm feeling pretty flattered, actually. This whole time I've been sure she sees me as a friend or just some asshole she's helping because she's a good person. Maybe I was wrong.

"I have no idea," she says. "But I think I need to go to bed before I say even more things I'll regret."

I'm still trying not to laugh. "Okay. Why don't you just show me where you keep a spare blanket and pillow, and then you can go to bed."

"Why do I need a spare blanket and pillow?" She sounds confused.

"*I* need a spare blanket and pillow. I'm sleeping here." I pat the couch between us and try not to grimace at the size. Or lack thereof. There's no way I'm going to fit on this, but I suppose it's better than sleeping at the hospital.

"That's really not necessary," she says.

"Yes it is. Clifford might come back and I'm not leaving you here alone."

This time she doesn't correct me about Cameron's name.

"Okay," she says, after a moment of internal deliberation.

She disappears down the hallway.

While she's gone, I start getting ready for bed, which includes removing my shoes and my shirt. I don't necessarily have to remove my clothing now, but...I'm curious after her last comment. I want to see her reaction.

I've got my back to the room, looking out the window and down into the parking lot when I hear her behind me.

When I turn around to face her, she's standing there with her eyes squeezed shut.

I can't help but grin.

"Here," she says, holding out the pillow and blanket blindly.

"You can open your eyes," I say. "I'm not naked."

"That's fine," she says, keeping her eyes closed.

I wait a second before taking the items from her, and she releases a breath before spinning around and stalking towards her room.

"Goodnight," she calls out when she's disappeared from view.

"Goodnight."

I hear a door shut softly and I turn and look down at the small couch with a sigh. It's going to be a long night.

I can't get comfortable. I just don't fit on this furniture and there's a spring digging into my back. I spend a couple hours alternating between staring up at the ceiling and looking out the window into the parking lot.

Around midnight, I hear muffled yelling and then outright screaming coming from Freya's bedroom.

I race into her room, heart thumping, only to find her in the middle of her bed, curled into a tense ball. I sit next to her and rub a hand down her back, not sure how to soothe her, or if I should wake her up.

"It's only a dream," I whisper, still rubbing her back.

This seems to work because some of the tension seeps away. After a few minutes, she relaxes back into sleep.

I carefully remove myself from the bed, resigned to heading back to the couch. Before I can move away, her hand flies out and grabs mine.

"Stay," she murmurs.

I'm not going to question the ethics of this decision. Not only will her bed actually fit my body, but curling up around her seems like the best idea I've ever had.

I slide into the bed behind her, one arm over her waist, her back fitting perfectly into my chest. She relaxes even more, the strain leaving her body until I hear her breathing even out and she's definitely sleeping.

This feels...good. Nice. Comfortable. I can't deny that I like having her body snug against mine, even if parts of me are waking up and straining against my boxers. Maybe it's not as complicated as I've been thinking. Maybe I can have a relationship and still take care of my family. I feel like

Freya would help me, not hinder me. Perhaps it would be easier with a partner and not harder.

And my mom is (probably) right.

I should be living with no regrets.

Finally, for the first time in what feels like days, I follow her into slumber.

16

Lawyers enjoy a little mystery, you know. Why, if everybody came forward and told the truth, the whole truth, and nothing but the truth straight out, we should all retire to the workhouse.

—Dorothy L. Sayers

Freya

I wake up the next morning surprised that I ever fell asleep. But I did. And I must have slept like the dead because my sheets are tangled around my legs, there's drool on my pillow, and there's another person in my bed.

I'm not drooling on my pillow, I'm drooling on *Dean*. Dean *is* my pillow.

My head snaps up and I stare at his face. He's still sleeping. Thank God.

Slowly, carefully, I lift my face off his chest and slide back slightly. Then I use the corner of the sheet to pat my drool off his chest. There. No harm done.

I put the sheet down, but I can't stop staring. Man, he's got a nice body.

He clears his throat.

My eyes jerk to his face. Crap.

He just smiles and says, "I had a dream I was being subjected to Chinese water torture, and I woke up with saliva on my chest."

"I have no idea how that might have happened."

He smiles and I smile and we sit there, smiling at each other until I realize I have no idea how or why he got in here in the first place.

"So...why are you, I mean, how did we—"

"You don't remember?" He lifts his head, bringing himself up on his elbows on the bed.

The motion brings his face too close to mine and I pull away.

"No," I say.

"You started screaming. I came running, you asked me not to leave, and I didn't argue since it's hard to sleep on a four-foot-long couch."

"Oh."

"You really don't remember any of that?" he asks, his eyes examining me intently.

I frown and shake my head again. "No."

Shit. What else did I say? Something embarrassing,

probably. I can't bring myself to ask. Instead, I slide away and out of the bed.

"I'm going to shower," I tell him, and then scurry down the hall and into the bathroom.

Am I ever going to have a night with the guy that doesn't end in mortification, or me acting like a moron?

I consider everything I know about myself. So, probably not.

When I flick on the light in the bathroom, I nearly shriek at my reflection. Oh God. How could Dean even stand to look at me like this? My hair is crazy, like, literally, sticking up in a million different directions of frizzy, wild rat's nest.

And my face...I forgot to wash up before bed. Raccoony would be an understatement. KISS would be more accurate.

I jump in the shower to tame the appearance and when I get out, I realize that I didn't bring any clothes with me.

Dammit.

This isn't happening. It's the biggest cliché ever: the girl getting out of the shower in nothing but a towel when the love interest bursts in. Could I be any more predictable?

I groan and sit on the toilet seat with my head in my hands. After my comments last night, and whatever happened to bring him to my bed, Dean is totally going to think I've got the hots for him. And I don't, I totally don't.

Shit. I do. I really do.

I slip out the door, past the kitchen and back into my bedroom.

Dean isn't there.

I frown. Did I pass him on my way in?

I meander back out to the living room, clutching the towel to my chest.

"Dean?" I call out.

Silence.

He left? Without saying anything? *Really?*

A brief pang of disappointment hits me right in the chest, and I immediately berate myself for allowing it.

Did I really expect anything else? I should be used to rude behavior. I just thought, after everything, that Dean was different.

I am such an idiot.

I go back to my room and change into skinny jeans, and a fitted T-shirt that says *Same Shirt, Different Day*.

I'm brushing out my hair when there's a knock at the door.

I peek out the peephole. Dean's on the other side.

I open the door and he walks in, arms full of grocery bags.

"What are you doing?"

"I went to get breakfast." He puts the bags on the counter while I shut the door and lock it behind him.

When I get to the kitchen, he's holding a package of bacon.

"Are you making bacon?" I ask.

He rummages through my drawers and then he turns around, spatula in hand. "Uh, yeah." He runs a hand through his hair. He seems a little nervous. "I hope you don't mind. I ran to the store and grabbed some stuff since I figured you would be hungry—"

I can't help it. I couldn't control myself if I tried. I take a few steps forward and throw my arms around his waist. He made me *bacon*.

"Um." I half hear and half feel him put the spatula on the counter behind him, and then his arms wrap around me.

"Thank you," I say.

"You're welcome." His arms wrap a little tighter around me. "Wow. You're really easy to please."

I pull away from him and look up into his face with a shrug. "Food makes me happy," I say.

"I sort of got that about you." He smiles down at me.

My hands are still on his waist. I pull them away and look at them like they're traitors.

"Uh," I say. Must change subject. "So, Lucy got into the police files—at least, part of them. She was able to confirm the time of death for both guys was around 11:00 p.m. and the same weapon was used for both killings, a nine-millimeter pistol."

"Oh," he says. He turns around and starts fiddling with the knobs on the stove.

"She also found out that Daisy, Jesse's girlfriend, was the one that reported you to the police as the boyfriend beater-upper and connected you to the homicides."

That stops him for a second. He turns to face me. "Really?"

"Yep."

I tell him about how Lucy and I went to verify Daisy's alibi, what the Natalie girl told us, and Lucy's suspicions while he keeps making the food. "Lucy's trying to hack into the campus security files now and see if she can access more of the police records. Hopefully, she'll find something useful. If Daisy went back to campus at some point in the evening, at least one of the cameras must have caught her, and that would totally disprove her signed statement. But we still can't find a connection between her and Matt."

His back is to me again, and he's flipping the bacon.

"Yeah." He doesn't sound happy. He pulls another pan out of the cupboard and clonks it on the stove.

"What do you think—"

"Look." He turns around. "I really appreciate what you guys are doing, and I hope that Lucy finds something to exonerate me, but..." He shakes his head. "I don't want to talk about it right now. I know it's important, but I want to have one day. Just one day where I don't think about what might happen, or who killed these guys. I have too much to worry about right now, I'm not sure I can take any more."

I pause for a second, absorbing his words. I get it, I do, but...

"What do you have to worry about that's more important than a murder charge?"

He shakes his head, turning around again and continuing to cook breakfast.

I didn't really expect him to answer my question, but it still irks me. What is he hiding? The fact that he's so secretive about everything just makes me want to know more.

I watch him flip pancakes like an expert as the silence extends and fills the space between us like the room is slowly filling with water. Just before I run out of air, I open my mouth.

"Wow. You're like a chef du jour."

The bacon is finished and he starts whipping up the eggs.

He glances over to frown at me. "Chef du jour translates into *chef of the day*. Am I the main course?"

An awkward pause while I think, *why, yes, maybe you are.*

For once, I manage to restrain myself. Instead I laugh. "Ha, ha...ha."

It comes out sounding fake and forced, which it is.

"Are you trying to feed my whole building or just us?"

"I know how much you eat. I came prepared."

"This is true. Do you need help?"

"I'm just about done. Why don't you grab the plates and the juice and set the table?"

I do as requested, setting my old vintage china on the small vinyl table in the corner of the kitchen along with silverware and glasses and the juice.

He brings out the plate of bacon, resting in a pile of paper towels. Then he grabs my plate and loads it with pancakes and eggs and brings it back to me.

"Syrup?" he asks.

I nod.

He brings that to the table, too.

Then he serves himself and sits in front of me.

I'm staring blankly at my full plate.

"Well," he says. "Dig in."

We're silent for a moment. He takes a bite and I've yet to even pick up my fork.

I feel one of his glares before I glance up and see it.

"Are you scared to eat my food or something?" he asks.

"It's not that," I say, shaking my head. "It's just that...no one's ever cooked for me before."

"What do you mean, no one's ever cooked for you before? That can't be true. Did you scavenge with wolves when you were a child?"

"No. But my mom's a vegan. We ate a lot of veggies and stuff from our garden when I was little, so I guess *scavenge* isn't entirely inaccurate."

I dump some syrup on my pancakes and dig in.

"Oh my God," I moan after taking a bite. "These are the best pancakes ever."

"No vegan pancakes while you were growing up?"

I shake my head no. "My mom's not exactly a cook. She'll make stuff like quinoa or veggie casserole, but when I got old enough to make my own food, I did. I'm not a very good vegan."

He looks pointedly down at my plate. Somehow half of the food is already in my stomach. "I can imagine you aren't. More eggs?"

"No, thanks." I smile at him.

There's a moment of silence, but it's not uncomfortable.

"So what about your parents?" I ask.

"What about them?"

"Did one of them teach you to cook like this?"

"Ah, sort of."

I point a finger at him. "Don't go being all secretive with me again. You always avoid my questions."

"I just don't like to talk about my parents."

My stomach plummets. "Oh God. Are they dead?

They're dead, aren't they?" I resist the urge to bang my head against the table. "I'm so nosy, I'm sorry!"

"No, they're not dead," he says and he sounds like he's stifling laughter.

"Oh, thank God," I say, relieved.

He doesn't elaborate any further and I don't want to keep grilling him about his personal life since he's obviously more than reluctant to share.

When we're done, he helps me clear the table and we do the dishes together.

"What are you doing today?" he asks when we're done and he's drying his hands on a towel.

It's Saturday. I had some grand plans that involved homework, a *Supernatural* marathon, and consuming the equivalent of my own body weight in popcorn and Reese's Pieces.

"I don't know." I shrug.

"No plans?" he asks, crossing his arms and leaning back against the counter.

"No plans. Why?"

"Can I take you somewhere?"

"Are you going to take me to your evil lair and have your wicked way with me?" I ask, with what might be a little too much enthusiasm.

"You wish." He smiles. Then he gets a little serious. He reaches out and takes one of my hands in his. "Come on. Come with me."

"Where are we going?"

"A couple of different places."

"Dude, you never tell me anything. Why do you have so many secrets?"

"Well, maybe today I'm going to show you some of my secrets."

"All of them?" I ask, like I won't go wherever it is he wants unless he's willing to divulge everything. But the truth is he had me as soon as his hand touched mine.

"Maybe."

"Okay."

He smiles and releases my hand. "Okay. Can I use your shower first?"

He's very prepared. He keeps a spare change of clothes in his car, so after retrieving his stuff and showering—I can't get the idea of him naked in my shower out of my mind—we take his car to wherever it is he's taking me.

"Are you going to tell me where we're going?" I ask after we've been driving for a few minutes.

"Nope."

"How long will it take to get there?"

"It's only about ten miles away."

"Okay, so the way you drive, it'll be an hour?" I laugh and he shoots me a dirty look.

"Very funny, Danica Patrick."

"Can we play twenty questions about where we're going?"

"Only if I reserve the right to not answer."

"You're such a buzzkill," I say, but his response doesn't stop me. "Will there be anyone else there?" I ask.

"Yes."

"Will they be old or young?"

"Both."

"Will there be food?"

He glances over at me with a frown. "We just ate enough to last three days."

"Well, I need to know these things so I can prepare myself mentally for the next time I can expect to eat."

"I think your mother damaged you by making you forage in the garden. You were a feral child and now you're a feral woman."

"You know what," I say after a moment's consideration. "You might be right."

He laughs as we pull up outside a small house in a neighborhood I've never been in. It's not a super ghetto neighborhood, but it's not quite middle class, either. The houses are old, the sidewalks full of cracks, and half the lawns we pass are full of weeds.

The garage is open at the house we stop in front of. It's stuffed with boxes and too much stuff to actually fit a car, but there is no car anyway. Just a bicycle that looks like it belongs to a kid.

He runs around and opens my door while I'm busy looking around.

"Where are we?" I ask as I get out of the car.

"My mom's," he says simply.

Then he takes my hand and leads me inside.

17

Everyone has their burdens, their grief, that they carry with them.

–Elizabeth Edwards

Freya

I have no time to prepare myself or badger him with more questions.

The house is small, but clean. When we walk in, there's an older Hispanic woman vacuuming and yelling at someone in the kitchen. I can't see who she's talking to because there's a wall in the way. As soon as she sees us, she stops the talking and the vacuum hums to silence.

She speaks rapid-fire Spanish to Dean before walking

over and taking him into a hug, still talking while kissing him on the cheeks.

He responds, speaking better Spanish than I ever could have imagined emerging from his mouth, then he introduces us. "This is Alejandra, she's my mom's neighbor and she comes over sometimes to help with stuff around the house."

"Mucho gusto," I say, one of the few Spanish phrases I remember from high school.

Alejandra grabs my hands and half holds, half shakes them, still talking and looking at me and then Dean and then back at me again. I have no idea what she's saying, and then she's hugging me. I look over at Dean, but he just shrugs. Then Alejandra is moving away, back into the kitchen, still talking quickly.

We follow her into the kitchen and that's when I see Dean's mom.

She's sitting in a chair at the small kitchen table. She has a light pink bandana over her clearly bald head. Her eyes are large in her thin face, her cheeks are sunken and her pallor is gray.

But she smiles when she sees Dean and her whole face lights up.

He immediately goes to her, leaning over and folding her into a hug.

"Dean, honey, what are you doing here? You never come over on Saturdays. Don't you have studying to do?"

He stands up and steps back so she can see me, hovering in the open doorway.

"I wanted you to meet my friend," he says.

I walk in and lean over and give her a hug, too. Everyone seems so touchy feely around here, and I am totally into that. But, you know, not in a creepy way.

"It's really nice to meet you, Mrs. Collins," I say, pleased that I remembered Dean's last name from when I got him out of the clink. Her shoulders feel thin and frail under my hands.

"Dean's told me so much about you," I continue. I turn around and give Dean a pointed look that I hope says something along the lines of, *you told me absolutely nothing, you ass, and I'm going to make you regret it.*

"He has?" His mom sounds surprised.

"Where's Sarah?" Dean asks, interrupting us.

"Sarah!" Alejandra yells so loud, I flinch and nearly have to cover my ears.

A door creaks open somewhere and the clomp of feet yammer down the hall in our direction. For a minute, I wonder if "Sarah" is a call for a herd of wild goats, but no. Sarah is a young girl, perhaps eleven or twelve. She's lanky with the same blue eyes and blonde hair as Dean.

As soon as she steps the threshold into the kitchen, Dean takes her in a headlock and noogies the top of her head.

"Hey, what?" Sarah immediately attempts to squirm out of the grasp of her older brother, lanky limbs flying.

Dean releases her and Sarah's red faced and obviously embarrassed by the laughter coming from the rest of the room.

"Sorry, sis," Dean says, slinging an arm around her

shoulder. “I can’t help it. I see you, and I just want to mess with you.”

Sarah groans and slaps a hand over her face. “Can I go back to Call of Duty now?” she asks.

“You’re letting her play that shit?” Dean asks his mom.

“Hey, language!” she says.

“Sorry.” Dean holds up his hands in supplication.

“You’re the one that bought her that Nintendo, or whatever it is.”

“Playstation,” Dean corrects.

“Whatever.” She waves her hand.

“Ugh, kids and their video games,” I say, pulling out the chair and sitting next to Dean’s mom.

“Right?” she says, nodding at me. “What’s your name? I’m sorry, but Dean hasn’t mentioned you until today.” She gives him a look that’s very similar to the look I just gave him.

“No worries.” I roll my eyes. “He’s such a boy. My name’s Freya.” I stick out my hand.

“You can call me Meredith, sweetie,” she says, taking my hand. “All that Mrs. Collins stuff makes me feel old,” she laughs. “Are you guys staying for lunch? Alejandra made a whole casserole dish of enchiladas.”

“We’d love to!” I say, at the same time Dean says, “We can’t.”

I shoot him another dirty look and then turn back to Mrs. Collins, er, Meredith.

“So,” I say, “do you have any embarrassing stories about Dean when he was a kid?”

An hour later, I'm sitting on a porch swing with Dean's mom, while he tosses a football with his sister on the lawn. Meredith spent the last hour showing me pictures of Dean when he was a kid, while he moaned and groaned and finally left our trash talk for the safety of his sister's room, but even he couldn't handle the video game warfare for long.

"Do you want some more ice tea?" his mom asks me.

"No, I'm good, thanks."

Just then, Dean laughs at something his sister said, throwing his head back before pitching the ball back at her in a clean spiral.

"I haven't seen him laugh like that in a long time," Meredith says.

"Really?" I ask. He seems to laugh a normal amount…at me, anyway. Well, I guess he used to be mostly grumpy, and now he's only sometimes grumpy.

"Nope." She shakes her head and sighs. "I hope you don't mind me oversharing, but when I got sick, Dean got very serious. It's my fault, really. There was so much I couldn't do anymore. I was too tired. Too sick. Too…not present."

"It's not your fault," I assure her. I pat her hand. "You couldn't stop yourself from getting sick."

"I know. But…it wasn't fair for Dean. He didn't have much of an adolescence, you know. It's not just that I got sick. I made bad decisions in relationships, and Dean paid the price. He grew up too fast. He didn't get to slow down and enjoy his youth. He suddenly had this huge responsibility, and in the process, he missed out on the best parts of his formative years."

Sarah yells something to Dean about being an old man and how she can totally kick his ass because he'll break a hip, and he laughs again.

"You're the first girl he's brought home in a long time," Meredith says.

"Oh. We're not—"

"Angelica was the last one, and this was over a year ago. She was too...cold. Serious. Sort of like him, but much worse."

I want to ask what she means, but I don't want to be too nosy.

She takes a sip of her tea. "You are full of life and spontaneity, I can tell these things."

Oh, if she only knew.

"I think you're a good influence on Dean. He's been unhappy for too long. This is the first time I've seen him have fun in years. Whatever you're doing, don't stop."

I stare into her serious, shadowed eyes for a few seconds before nodding. "Okay," I say.

18

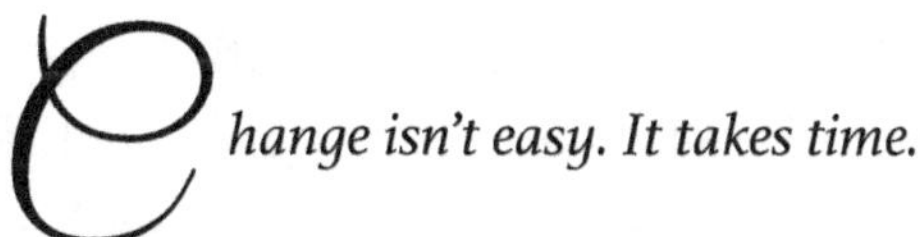

Change isn't easy. It takes time.

—Caroline Kennedy

Dean

After we've eaten enchiladas and cleaned up the kitchen, Mom goes to lie down, but not before telling me to take Freya out in the backyard and show her the flowers I planted.

"She's going through her third round of chemo," I say, leaning over to pick a weed out of the dirt.

A cloud goes over the sun and I see Freya shiver out of the corner of my eye.

I shove my hands in my pockets. "We'll find out soon if she can stop, or if we need to do more aggressive therapy."

There's a few red tulips blooming in a flower box along the fence line.

Freya reaches out and brushes one with a finger. She doesn't say anything, so I continue.

"The first time she had breast cancer, I was just a kid. They had to perform a complete mastectomy. Then she was in a car accident a couple years ago and hurt her shoulder, and the cancer came back and attached to her injury. This time is harder than the others. She still works. Her boss has been very cool since she's out of it most of the time. She does clerical tasks, and she doesn't make much—enough to allow her to keep her insurance. But the insurance doesn't cover everything and she's gotten to the point where she can't drive so I pay for a taxi to take her to and from work. I also help with Sarah's clothes, food, the mortgage...whatever they need."

I don't look at her. I don't really want to see her reaction. Instead, I keep my gaze focused on the flowers.

"This is why you do what you do and live where you live," she murmurs.

"Yeah," I say.

I brace myself for her response. I don't typically tell people what's happening with my family, because I don't know how they'll react. I've had bad experiences with that. I don't like to make people feel uncomfortable or sorry for me. It is what it is. It's no one's fault and I can only do the best I can.

She comes up to my side and slides an arm around my waist. "I'm sorry," she says.

She doesn't sound pitying or uncomfortable. I hug her back, pulling her against me.

"It's nobody's fault," I say. "Things happen."

"Shit happens," she says. "It sucks."

"True. This is why I have a hard time focusing on...everything else. When I think about what might happen to my mom and sister if they actually charge me with something..." I trail off and clear my throat before continuing. "They have enough to worry about. I don't want them worrying about me. And if I'm sent away, who will take care of them?"

"I would," she says quickly.

I pull away slightly and look down at her. Her eyes are bright and she's staring at me, and I realize I believe her. I trust her. It's been so long since I trusted anyone other than my family. "You would, wouldn't you?" I ask.

"But I won't have to because we'll get to the bottom of it and you won't be charged with anything."

We're silent for a moment, just standing there in the spring breeze. After a few seconds, I step back.

"Are you ready to get out of here? There's somewhere else I want to take you."

She nods.

We go back inside. Mom's still asleep, so we say goodbye to Sarah and get back in the car.

"Where are we going now? Another surprise?" she asks, clicking her seat belt into place.

"It's not far," I say.

"Okay, Mr. Mystery."

We drive less than a mile before pulling into a small lot next to a park that's seen better days. There's one lonely swing swaying in the breeze, a slide, and a small merry-go-round that looks like it was red at one time, but now is mostly gray because a majority of the paint has chipped off.

There's a large expanse of dead grass, and beyond that, trees that continue into the distance. A cloud passes over the sun, making the park underneath it even more gloomy and depressing.

"Come on," I say. We get out of the car and she follows me.

We walk through the tired playground, across the grass and into the trees. There's a small deer path winding through the woods, and we clomp down it.

"Now you really are taking me to your lair, aren't you?" she teases.

"Maybe." I take her hand and help her climb over a fallen tree trunk.

"Who's Angelica?" she asks when we're winding down the small path. It's too narrow to walk side by side, so I'm leading.

I glance back at her. "What?" I heard her, but I'm stalling because I don't want to answer.

"Angelica," she repeats, a little louder. "Your mom mentioned that you haven't brought a girl home since Angelica. Who was she? A girlfriend?"

I shake my head. "I don't want to talk about it."

"Fine. But just so you know, I'm taking that picture of

you in the tub with that other boy that your mom showed me, and I'm distributing copies around campus."

I laugh. "I was two."

"Doesn't matter."

"I thought you'd given up vengeance."

"This isn't vengeance, it's blackmail," she corrects.

"Ah, my mistake."

The trees peter out, and as they gradually disappear the sound of rushing water gets louder. We step around the last tree and into a large meadow. She follows me through the waist-high grass. Our movements disturb a big gray bird that takes off into the distance.

I lead her to a wide, flat area where the grass is short and soft. There's more tall grass around us, and the creek is on the other side. I can hear it clearly, even though I can't see it. This is where we stop.

"What are we doing here?" she asks.

"I used to come here a lot as a kid," I say with a shrug. "I wanted you to see it."

"It's beautiful," she says.

I cross my arms over my chest and scuff my foot on the ground. "I also thought this would be a good place to show you a few things."

"Like what?"

"I'm a little worried about this whole thing with Carter." I rub my chin and avoid her eyes.

"Cameron. And yeah, you and me both."

"I can't be around you all the time."

"Geez, am I that annoying?" she asks.

I chuckle and shake my head. "No, not that. I'm

worried that if I'm not around he'll show up and try something with you. I want to show you a few defense moves."

"You're going to teach me self-defense?"

"Some."

"Are you qualified to instruct me on this?"

"Does a black belt in karate qualify me?"

"No wonder you've got the body of a Greek god and can break grown men in two." She gapes at me.

I have to smile at that. "Greek god, huh?"

She flushes and closes her eyes. "Why don't I have a filter?"

"It's no biggie," I say to spare her further embarrassment. "I've been doing karate since I was a kid."

"If you say so, Iron Man."

"Iron Man? I thought I was Thor."

"You can be whoever I want you to be."

I sigh. "Okay. Let's start with the basics."

I show her how to react to different attacks, from the front, from the back and from the side. Since she's short, I teach her how to use the lower center of gravity to her advantage.

She has a hard time at first, but quickly gets into the practice combat. It's never easy to attack or fight back if you've never done it before.

I also show her simple ways to inflict pain, by pulling fingers in opposite directions and twisting the skin on the arm. Very little pressure, but immediately painful.

The hardest part is when I have her on the ground on her back and I'm lying on top of her. Her breathing changes and I can tell she's just as affected as I am by the position.

"I'll give you twenty minutes to stop doing this," she says when I pin her hands at her side.

I frown down at her. "This is serious," I say. "If you get to this point with someone, you're going to have very limited options on how to break out of it."

"I'm well aware of *that*," she mutters.

"What does that mean?"

"Nothing," she says.

I roll off and to the side and lie in the grass next to her.

For a brief moment, the clouds break and the sun shines through. I look over at Freya and she's shut her eyes against the glare.

I shift closer to her, letting my shoulder brush hers as I turn onto my side, leaning on my elbow, head in hand.

She turns her head, opening one eye to squint at me.

"Tell me," I say.

"Tell you what?"

"Don't play dumb, Freya. You're continually making these cryptic references, and I know it has something to do with your relationship with Colin."

"Cameron," she mumbles.

She sits up a little and turns towards me so we are both on our sides, facing each other. She mimics my pose, head in hand, elbow on the ground. "Why should I tell you anything?" she asks. "You won't tell me anything about this Angelica person. You totally surprised me with your mom, without saying a word, and you expect me to be all, *oh yes, let me tell you all my dark secrets,*" she says in a higher-pitched voice before continuing in a regular tone. "Even though you're always glaring at me and won't tell me shit for shit."

She flops back, arms crossing over her chest.

I hate it that she's right.

"Fine," I say, rolling onto my back and staring up at the sky. At some point, the sun disappeared behind the clouds again.

"Angelica was my girlfriend. We met in high school, and we were together for three years. When Mom got sick again, things changed. I had to cut back on everything in order to help her pay for her medical bills, and Angelica wasn't exactly supportive. I didn't realize how materialistic she was until I stopped taking her out and buying her things. She couldn't handle being around my mom. She said it made her too sad to see her that way, but I think the truth was..." I stop on a sigh. "It was like she thought cancer was something dirty people get. I don't know. She came from money. Her family and upbringing were so different than mine."

"Sounds like a heinous bitch," she says.

I laugh and look over at her disgusted expression. "Yeah. She wasn't like you, all bleeding heart and fighting the man."

She doesn't say anything but her disgusted face morphs into a smile for me.

"Your turn," I say, rolling over to face her again.

She opens her eyes and rolls in my direction to face me. This puts us very close together. All I would have to do is lean forward slightly...

"My turn for what?" she asks, playing stupid.

I give her a look and try not to smile. "Don't play coy with me."

"I'm not playing anything."

"I just spilled about my terrible relationship. You never told me what happened with Colby other than the cheating, and I'm not buying that that's the end of that story. He's too much of an ass."

She doesn't respond. She stares at me for a moment, looking thoughtful. Then her gaze moves from my eyes to my lips and my mouth goes dry. All I can think about is kissing her. Pulling her bottom lip into my mouth.

She looks like I feel.

There's only a thin band of air separating our bodies.

"Why are you looking at me like that?" I ask. My voice sounds rough and slightly lower than usual.

"Like what?"

"You're looking at me the same way you look at food," I say.

Her eyes move up to mine. "Do you feel as if your life's in danger?"

"I've seen what you do with your food. I'm terrified."

She leans forward and kisses me. It's not much of a stretch, with our lips only inches away. I reach out to pull her closer, but it's over before I can make contact. She pulls back and rolls to her feet.

I miss her immediately.

"Where are you going?" I ask from the ground.

"To cool off," she says, heading towards the water.

I have to take a moment to compose myself and my

pants before following after her. The creek is only a dozen feet away, hiding behind the tall grass.

I find her standing at the edge of the small embankment, looking down at the water.

"Are you going to cool off?" I ask.

"No."

"Why not?"

She looks over at me with a smile. "I don't swim."

I frown and look down at the water skeptically. "You don't need to know how to swim. This isn't more than a foot wide and two inches deep."

"Oh, no. I know *how* to swim. It's not that I *can't*, it's that I *don't*. I don't like to swim in anything other than a pool."

"Why not?"

"Jaws."

I laugh and rub the back of my head with my hand, deciding to play along with her ridiculousness. "I'm pretty sure Jaws can't fit in there."

"You never know."

I shove her gently in the shoulder, making her trip forward, her sandal making a loud *plop* sound in the shallow water.

"Hey!" she yells.

"Don't worry, fair maiden!" I proclaim, stepping into the water after her. "I will rescue you!" I grab her arms, pulling her up onto the other side of the small stream.

"Thank God." She clutches at me. "I thought for sure I would drown."

"It's a good thing I was here." I smile down at her. It's been a long time since I've let myself be silly and not worry about what's going to happen tomorrow. Not since I was a kid. Before Mom got sick.

She grins up at me, and I can't help what happens next.

I bend down and kiss her, keeping my lips gentle, and pulling her small frame into mine so we are flush together. Her lips are quite possibly the sweetest thing I've ever tasted. I try to take it slow and enjoy the moment, but at some point, it changes. The motion of our mouths progresses from slow and gentle to intense and almost rough, so much so that I barely notice when we move from standing to lying down on the soft grass embankment.

The next thing I know, she's half underneath me and one of my legs slides between hers. She reacts by arching herself into me, making my breath falter and even more blood rush southward. My hand slides down her side and I squeeze her hip. Her skin is impossibly soft.

And then it happens. She tenses and stops breathing. I pull away to see what's wrong, and I watch it come over her like a wave. Her breath bursts suddenly from her lungs in quick spurts and I help her sit up and put her head between her legs.

After a moment of sitting there with me rubbing her back and murmuring words that mean nothing, her breathing returns to nearly normal.

"What happened?" she asks.

"You had a panic attack."

"I did?"

"Yes."

"How do you know that?"

"It's happened to me before."

"Oh."

She sits up and looks at me. Her face is flushed and a sheen of sweat glistens on her forehead.

I must look concerned, because she pats me on the knee. "I'm okay," she says. "Mortified beyond belief, which must be shocking to you considering our history together has been chock-full of me being an idiot, but I'm still okay."

I don't say anything. I know there has to be a reason she panicked, and I imagine the reason is a goddamn douchenugget named Cameron.

But I know she won't talk about it, even if I ask. Finally, I say, "Let's get you home."

19

The most difficult crime to track is the one which is purposeless.

–Arthur Conan Doyle

Freya

I can't believe that just happened. I was making out with a hot dude, and I totally lost my shit.

I don't know if it's because we were lying down, or because the kiss had morphed into crazy passion, but something started building in my chest. It was like a balloon, expanding, pounding, pressing against my lungs and making it harder to draw in air. I couldn't breathe.

One second, Dean and I were kissing and touching and

melting into each other like snow on hot asphalt, and then next thing I knew, I was sitting up and he was rubbing my back, my head between my legs, heart pounding and chest burning.

In a word, horrifying.

I glance over at him while he's driving. It's been a quiet ride home. He must think I'm a total fool. I *am* a total fool.

And he's…so not a fool. The more I get to know him, the more I realize that Dean is the antithesis of Cameron. The way he takes care of his mom and sister. So different from what I would have expected.

It makes sense now, why he's always grumpy. I guess I would be grumpy too if my mom was sick and had no one to support her but me, and I was trying to go through college while participating in illegal activities to make ends meet not just for myself, but for an entire family.

The drive home ends quickly since I spent most of it lost in self-loathing.

He parks in the lot next to my car.

It's immediately apparent that every single window of my vehicle has been smashed to bits.

"What the hell happened here?" he asks.

"How am I supposed to know? I've been with you all day!"

He gets out of the car, slamming his door, and stalks around my vehicle. "Stay." He points his finger at me.

Oh, no, I am not a dog. He cannot tell me to stay. I immediately open my door and follow him while he examines the damage.

"Someone shot through this window," he says.

I peer at the window, standing behind him. There's a small circular hole surrounded by a spider web of cracked glass. I scratch my head. "With a gun?"

He gives me a look. "What else would they shoot with?"

"Sorry, it's just...why would anyone want to shoot out my windows?"

"I'm guessing that Corey is venting his anger at you."

"*Cameron* has no reason to be angry at me. We broke up months ago."

"Well, I can't think of anyone else who would do this to you. Unless you have an enemy you aren't telling me about?"

"What? No. I am universally loved."

He gives me another look.

"Okay. Maybe I'm universally tolerated."

He nods and turns back around, shading his eyes to peer inside the windows.

"What are you looking for?"

"The bullet. Your friend Lucy said Matt and Jesse were both shot with a—"

A loud crack splits the air, echoing around us. The next thing I know, I'm slammed into the ground on my back, Dean's body hovering over mine.

"Ow! You hurt my butt, you jerk."

"Someone is shooting at us."

"That's ridiculous, you're losing your mind. No one is shooting at us, it was just a car backfiring."

There's another loud pop and the window we were just looking through shatters completely, bits of glass flying all over us.

"It shattered this way," Dean whispers. He's still hovering over me, our legs entangled, trying to keep his body weight from crushing me underneath him, his face only inches away from mine.

Perhaps there really is someone shooting at us.

"So?"

He seems remarkably calm, and I am freaking the eff out.

"That means they're on the other side of the car. Maybe on the other side of the street or hiding behind some of the construction equipment." He slides off of me and sits with his back to my tire, motioning for me to do the same. I roll over, cutting my hands on glass against the black top before scooting over to the opposite tire and sticking my head between my legs.

This can't be happening. This doesn't happen in real life. This only happens in the movies, or to people who live in big cities with ghettos and gangs and things that only exist on TV. Not in front of my quiet little apartments!

"Do you have your cell on you?" Dean asks while he's trying to peek over the hood in the direction the shots are coming from.

"It's in your car." I motion towards it.

He crab walks over to his vehicle, ass in the air, and I'm struck with an irrational and overwhelming urge to laugh. I feel a hysterical bubble rising and clap my hands over my mouth.

Staying down on his knees, he opens the car door and reaches inside for the phone. "If you laugh…" I can tell he's trying to be serious but there's a thread of laughter in his voice. "I swear to God, woman."

"I find that I'm frequently avoiding the urge to laugh at the most inappropriate times."

He's got my phone now. He crab walks back to me, and now I'm really laughing.

"Why is that, do you think?" he asks, dialing 9-1-1 into the phone before pressing it against his ear.

"I'm sure Lucy would be able to give us a scientific explanation. Probably has something to do with nerves and my body's reaction to stressful situations."

"Yes, hi, I need to report an active shooter," Dean says into the phone when someone answers on the line.

"They're going to send Tweedle-dum and Tweedle-dumber, aren't they?" I mutter while he's giving the operator our location and an update on what's happening.

"With your luck," Dean says, holding a hand over the mouthpiece, "absolutely."

By the time the cavalry arrives, the shooter is nowhere to be found. A police officer searches both of us and the vehicles, lights are shone in our eyes, and we have to fill out statements. At Dean's insistence, I mention Cameron the douche in my statement and write about how he came over the night before and acted threatening.

Once all of that's done and we've stood around forever, a detective comes over to ask us questions.

This time, it's not the two yahoos that interrogated

Dean; instead, it's a woman. She looks young, not much older than us. Her hair is pulled back into a no-nonsense bun, and she's dressed casually in jeans, a white shirt and a leather jacket. I wouldn't have pegged her as a cop except for the badge stuck to her jeans.

"Hi," she says sticking out her hand. "I'm Detective Hanson."

"Dean," he says shaking her hand.

"Freya." I shake her hand, too, and then step back and stand closer to Dean.

"I heard from Miller and Stevens that you are being questioned in connection with two separate counts of homicide."

Dean nods.

Miller and Stevens must be the other detectives that were questioning Dean after Matt died.

"Have you two heard of Devil's Gate?"

"As in the doorway to hell?" I ask.

"Pretty much. It's a new drug going around, a very powerful hallucinogen. There's been a rash of crimes around the university and this drug might play a part. There was a similar shooting last week, and we think these two incidents may be related."

She's watching Dean as she speaks.

"I don't do drugs," he says.

"If you were, maybe, selling these drugs, that would give someone ample motive to be shooting at you to get to it. It's highly addictive."

"I don't sell drugs," Dean says.

She nods. "It's obvious neither of you are using. This

drug makes people crazy. Jittery, paranoid. It also makes your pupils dilate like you wouldn't believe. However, I did read in your file that you refused a search of your apartment." She shrugs and smiles at us disarmingly. "Some might think you have something to hide."

"I don't sell drugs," Dean insists.

"Okay." She holds up her hands and steps away from us. "Some advice? If you are hiding something, you might want to confess and make a deal. You could get your charges reduced if you offer information to help us squash the people dealing this drug. And I recommend sooner rather than later. It's bad enough to have homicide on your ass, you don't want to add vice breathing down your neck. We make very bad bedfellows."

Then she spins on her boot and walks away.

Once we're able to get away from all the fuzz and we're safely ensconced in my apartment, I call Lucy to tell her what's going on.

I get about two sentences in when she interrupts with, "I'm coming over," and hangs up on me.

While we're waiting, Dean grabs a first-aid kit from his car for the cuts on my hands. I sit on the counter in the kitchen and he stands in front of me, taking one hand at a time and gently cleaning the dirt out.

I watch his tender ministrations in silence.

When he's finished bandaging both hands, instead of letting go, he rubs a gentle finger against the inside of my wrist. I stare down at where his hand meets mine. The unexpected touch makes my breath catch in my throat. I meet his gaze and find his bright blue eyes focused intently on mine.

In one swift movement, before I can even register what he's all about, he steps between my legs, cups my face in his hands and presses his lips against mine.

After a couple seconds, he pulls away. "Sorry," he says, stepping away, his eyes on the floor.

"Why are you sorry?" I ask.

He runs a hand through his hair and meets my eyes. "I shouldn't have done that, not after what happened earlier."

I reach out and grab his hand, pulling him a little closer. "It's okay," I say.

He steps towards me, watching my face, and I know he wants me to tell him why I freaked. And I know he deserves an explanation.

"Will you tell me—" he starts, but there's a loud knock at the door.

"Lucy," I say. I hope off the counter and scoot around Dean to let her in.

It's not just Lucy at the door; Jensen is with her. I make introductions all around, and then we sit in the living room and talk over everything that's happened. Minus the make-out sessions, I don't think that's relevant to the crime, although Dean is criminally hot, so there is that.

Halfway into the shooting story, Lucy begins pacing back and forth in front of us in the narrow space between my coffee table and the TV.

"Who was their target, I wonder," she murmurs when I finish telling the story. "Freya or Dean?"

I'm not sure she's actually asking us anything, she's more talking to herself.

"We need to start at the beginning." She stops suddenly and turns towards us. "Let's make a timeline of events. Jesse was killed first. We have Daisy as a potential suspect. Five days later, Matt was killed. Same murder weapon, same general location." She starts her pacing again. "Today, shots were fired into Freya's car. Again, we think it's the same type of gun. They haven't confirmed the bullets came from the same weapon. I imagine it will take a few days to get that information from the lab. The vice detective said that another shooting happened involving a strong narcotic that's been going around campus. What's the connection?"

She stops, facing us.

I consider the connections between myself and the victims. "Daisy could have been doing drugs—she and her friends seem like party animals. But, as far as I know, there's no connection between us. Well, Liz the slut is a connection for me to Matt, but Jesse...nothing."

"Maybe the shots were meant for Dean." Jensen motions to him. "You are a connection between the two."

"But who would want to shoot me?" Dean asks. "Daisy? And why?"

"I did discover that Daisy's brother owns a variety of firearms," Lucy says. "He's a hunter and an active member of the NRA and Ducks Unlimited."

"Ducks Unlimited?" I ask.

"It's a non-profit organization that works to conserve

wetlands and habitat for various fowl and wildlife. They also promote the continuation of safe and regulated hunting of the aforementioned animals. So, she has access to firearms."

Dean clears his throat before speaking. "She had the means, the motive—for Jesse—and the perfect person to throw under the bus once Matt died." He stops for a second before saying, "Do you think she killed Matt for the sole purpose of implicating me? Although, why would she do that if she already had a solid alibi? Solid enough for the police, anyway."

"Maybe she recognized that her alibi was shaky and was looking for an insurance policy?" I try.

Lucy frowns. "None of it makes sense. She might think her alibi needed work if she knew we were digging around —it might make sense for her to target Freya. But what about me? I was with Freya when we went to talk to Daisy's friend, and I haven't received threats of any nature." She shakes her head. "I need more information. Maybe there's another connection we aren't aware of. I was able to download half of the video files surrounding the areas where the murders occurred on campus. Once I view them, I might have more information as early as next week."

"Next week is spring break," Dean says.

"We'll be in town," Jensen says.

"I'm going to my mom's," I say.

"Like hell you are," Dean tells me.

"Are you bossing me around again? Because you know how well that works out for you." I cross my arms over my chest.

Jensen stands and grabs Lucy's hand. "We should probably get going."

"You're not going anywhere alone until we've figured out who's shooting at you and they're safely behind bars," Dean says to me.

Lucy pats him on the shoulder. "Good point," she says before turning in my direction. "He's right. You shouldn't drive by yourself around town, let alone eight hours on the road. We don't know who the shots were intended for, but the fact that they shot at your car provides a high indication that it was you. Plus, you probably won't be able to replace all the windows before you have to leave, so a free ride might be a good idea."

I hate it when she's right.

"I could rent a car," I say, raising my eyebrows at Dean.

Lucy sighs and rolls her eyes. "Dean, call me if you need help with this one," she tells him before walking over to give me a hug.

I hear Jensen and Dean talking to each other, exchanging goodbyes, but I'm more focused on Lucy.

"Why are you on his side? You're supposed to be *my* friend!"

"He's concerned about your safety. That means he cares about you. Why don't you consider letting him?"

"Fine." There's no point in arguing with her, especially since she's always right. Well, almost always. "Call me at my mom's if you find anything."

"I will."

Once they leave, Dean and I stare at each other for a brief moment across the living room.

"So," he says, shoving his hands in his pockets and looking down at the ground. "We should probably stay at my place tonight." He looks up to meet my eyes. "I have more security and since the shooting happened here, it will probably be safer there...what do you think?"

"You're asking instead of commanding?"

He pulls one hand from his pocket to run it through his hair. "I don't mean to be bossy. I'm just used to taking care of people."

And with that little reminder of who he's been taking care of and supporting for years, my anger deflates. "Fine," I say. "Let me get a bag together."

I move to walk past him, but he stretches out and pulls me into a hug. "I'm sorry," he says, resting his head on top of mine.

"Me too," I say, reaching my hands around his waist. "I don't mean to fight with you, I think I'm just stressed and tired. And probably hungry."

He laughs and the sound rumbles in my ear. "*Probably* hungry?" he asks.

"I'm like an infant. If I'm not fed and burped regularly I get cranky."

"Duly noted. We can pick up something on the way back to my place. Your choice."

I lean back and look up. I can't help but smile at him. "See. This is why I lo-ike you."

Jesus, I almost just said I love you to Dean. Out loud. And it was totally obvious that I changed it to like at the last minute. Who says I *loike* you? I can feel my face heating. I push away from him and turn away.

"I'll be right back," I say, my back to him as I'm heading into my room.

I stuff some clothes into an overnight bag and zip it up.

I really need to pull it together. I know it's just a commonly thrown around phrase, the whole, "I totally love you man," but after everything else that's happened with Dean and me, the last thing we need is to complicate matters.

Friends. Dean and I can be friends.

Dean can be my friend that I'm attracted to and want to make out with all the time.

I slap myself in the forehead.

"You okay in there?" Dean calls from the living room.

I can do this. "Yeah, coming."

20

It is a curious thought, but it is only when you see people looking ridiculous that you realize just how much you love them.

—Agatha Christie

Freya

"You really don't have to do this," I say for probably the forty-seventh time since Dean insisted on driving with me to my mom's house for spring break. "We'll be gone the whole week. What about your mom?"

He takes my suitcase from me and throws it in the trunk. "She's fine."

"What about your sister?"

"She's fine too." He slams the trunk.

"What about—"

"Look, just stop fighting it. I'm not letting you drive eight hours by yourself with people shooting at you. Don't make me call Lucy."

He opens the passenger door to his car, parked by the curb. He's hardly left me alone since the whole shooting thing, making me stay at his place and only dropping me off early this morning to pack before returning for me after running some errands he had to take care of before we left.

"They were probably shooting at you," I say.

"Then why did they bust up *your* car?"

"Probably because I've been hanging out with *you*."

He crosses his arms over his chest, his gaze drifting to the ground where he scuffs his foot against a bit of grass struggling to grow through the cracked pavement. "There might be some truth to that," he says finally before looking back up at me. "But, too late now. Get in the car."

"Ugh," I groan. "When will you stop ordering me around?"

"Maybe when you stop fighting with me at every turn."

I slide into the passenger seat. "I'm getting in," I say. "But not because you told me to."

"I'm sure that's true," he mutters, shutting my door for me and jogging around the front of the car to the driver's side.

Within minutes we're on the freeway, heading out of town.

"I gave Lucy my mom's number, because we probably won't have cell service at her house. She'll let us know if she finds anything." I plug an adaptor into the cigarette lighter hole. "I brought some music," I say, plugging it into my iPod.

"This better not be some girly shit."

"I don't listen to anything that can be described as coming out of an asshole."

He gives me a bemused smile before returning his attention to the road.

"I made you a playlist," I say, scrolling through my music. I find what I'm looking for and hit play. "This is totally your jam."

"Why is this my song?" he asks, after the words have filled the car and it's apparent the singer doesn't like anything.

"Because you hate everything."

"I do not."

"Maybe you don't hate everything, but you definitely hate me."

"I don't hate you."

"Right," I scoff.

"I don't. Who sings that, anyway?"

I switch over to the real playlist I made and Led Zeppelin's "Going to California" filters through the speakers.

"That was Ugly Kid Joe. 'Everything About You.' It's from like forever ago. And maybe hate is a strong adjective, but you definitely don't act like you like anything, either."

He changes lanes to pass a slow-moving vehicle and

once he's back in the other lane, he says, "I don't hate you. I've never been mean to you."

"Uh, whatever, liar. What about yelling at me this morning?"

"That wasn't yelling, that was loudly stating my opinion that you should not be driving long distance by yourself when there's a murderer on the loose who may or may not be trying to kill you."

"Pshhh, whatever."

We don't speak for a little while, listening to Robert Plant sing about a girl with love in her eyes and flowers in her hair.

"I'm just...not good at letting people get close," he says.

"Because of Angelica?"

He shrugs. "Maybe. Or maybe I've just witnessed a full history of crappy relationships."

He doesn't elaborate and I don't feel like pushing it. I have a feeling, based on what his mom said at his house, that he's talking about her relationships. I stare out the window, watching the miles pass by, listening to the music and the hum of the tires against the road.

A few hours later, I see a familiar sign.

I sit up straighter in my seat. "Hey," I say.

"What?"

"Can we stop at the fair?"

The sign is worn and old, the bright red color long since faded, but you can still read the words: "Orangeberry Fair! A year-round attraction! Good times two miles ahead!" I've always loved that sign because all the O's have smiley faces and there's a picture of a penguin in the corner. The penguin is completely random and has nothing to do with anything, but that's why I love it.

"I don't think we have time for that."

"What? Everybody got time for that! We left at the ass crack of dawn. We can stop for a couple hours and still get to my mom's by dinner. This is great, you're gonna love it. It's a year-round attraction. There's rides and games and one of those restaurants where you can sing karaoke and drop your peanut shells on the floor. I've always wanted to go, but my mom wouldn't let me because there's no vegan alternatives available."

He gives me a sideways glance that doesn't bode well for my chances of convincing him to stop.

"Please? Please, please, pretty please?" I give him my best pouty look. "I'll win you one of those giant stuffed animals," I bribe.

"Oh, well if you're going to give me a stuffed animal..."

"You mean we can go? We can really, really go?"

He lets out a loud, exaggerated sigh. "I guess so."

"Yes!" I squeal and try to hug him, but since he's driving that doesn't work out so well and he pushes me away saying something about hugging and driving not being safe. I'm so excited I don't even hear half the words coming out of his mouth.

He turns into a giant graveled parking lot a couple of miles later and I jump out of the car, dragging him towards the entrance after he takes about a million years locking up the car.

The park isn't terribly crowded since it's still fairly early in the day. Some families are wandering around, and there's a couple groups of teenagers. We pass through a line of booths selling various items like clothes, arts and crafts, and jewelry. We get wristbands to go on as many rides as we want and I make Dean do the strongman game, where you slam a giant hammer down on a lever and try to ring the bell at the top. I take pictures because, hey, it's Thor with a mighty hammer. He glares at my enthusiasm, but he still plays along and manages to ring the bell.

"My hero!" I exclaim when he hands me a giant stuffed armadillo.

After we've ridden all the twirly stuff, the droppy stuff, the Ferris wheel and the merry-go-round, it's close enough to lunch time that I feel justified dragging him into the food establishment in the center of the fair.

The restaurant is pretty packed, with people eating and crowding around the bar, enjoying the karaoke. We have to wait a few minutes to get a seat, and during that time we listen to a young girl's rendition of "Let it Go," and an inebriated guy sing "Baby Got Back."

There's a small stage for the singers, with a small TV facing them that displays the lyrics. There's a much larger projection screen facing the audience, which also shows the lyrics so the crowd can join in.

"Are you going to sing?" Dean asks after we're seated.

"Nah, I don't want to make people's ears bleed."

"You can't be that bad."

"Oh, I'm bad. I'm so bad that when I start singing, small children weep and grown men die where they stand."

After we order our food, I go to use the bathroom and put in a request with the DJ.

Lunch is excellent: large plates full of BBQ, mac and cheese, and criss-cross cut fries. A few more people sing while we eat, and the crowd really gets into the performances, laughing, clapping, booing and generally carrying on.

After we've finished our meal and paid, I'm trying to pick meat out of my teeth when it happens.

"Next up," the DJ calls on his microphone, "We've got Dean Collins!"

A smattering of applause flicks around the room and Dean gives me the death glare level ten.

"No," he says, shaking his head firmly. "No way." He looks kinda pale.

"Dean, where are you buddy?" The DJ says.

He's staring at me like he might puke, and I can't help grinning at him before yelling, "He's over here!" I start clapping and wooting and hollering.

Some of the crowd gets into it, whooping along with me.

He looks terrified. I can't help but laugh.

His jaw firms and he stands. As he passes me, heading for the stage he leans down and whispers in my ear, "You will pay for this."

In return, I smack him on the ass as he walks away. "Go get 'em, tiger!"

When he gets up to the stage, there's a slight pause before the song I picked out for him starts playing. He stands there, an immobile giant. Then the guitar begins bumping gently in the background, and the lyrics fill the screen behind him.

At first, Dean's a little slow to pick up the lyrics, and then he has to speed to catch up. He sounds nervous, his voice breaks a little at one of the words, and for a second I feel bad forcing him into this, but then something changes. The crowd starts cheering him on, offering encouragement. And his voice gets stronger and more confident, and then he gets to the chorus.

But I would walk five hundred miles...

More voices join his.

I look around, speechless, at the people in the crowd, the people at the tables, the people at the bar, most of whom are singing along.

This must give him confidence because he really starts getting into it, even rocking his head and body to the beat.

Then...

Da dat da! Da dat da!

Da-da-da dun-diddle un-diddle un-diddle un da-da

And I swear to God, the entire place has joined in at this point, the *da dat da's* are so loud, I can't hear my own laughter over the crowd.

When I get ahold of myself, I join in too.

Too soon, it's over, and the crowd gives Dean a standing ovation full of catcalls and whistles. I might be jealous, if the lady in the front row giving Dean the eye wasn't about eighty-five years old and missing most of her teeth.

He bows formally, laughing, before exiting the stage and beelining for our table.

"Let's get out of here," he says.

I worry for a second that he's mad, but his eyes are

bright and he seems happy and pumped up from the adrenaline rush.

"What, you don't want to stay and chat with all your adoring fans?" I ask. I glance behind him, but it seems the crowd has already moved onto the next act. Ah, the fleeting bliss of fame.

"I'm pretty sure the old lady in the front row was trying to take off her bra and throw it at me." He grimaces and rubs his chest. "I feel so violated."

"You sure? You wanna stick around and see if you have a chance? I'll be your wingman." I elbow him.

"Tempting...but no." He grabs my hand and leads me out of the restaurant while random strangers high-five him on the way out.

Then we're weaving through the throngs of people outside where the fair has gotten busier.

"Who sings that song?" he asks me as we trudge out the main entrance.

"The Proclaimers," I tell him. "They're Scottish."

It takes a few minutes to get back to the car, and he keeps my hand in his the whole time, even when the crowd thins and there's no reason to keep hanging on. Occasionally, his thumb rubs against my palm, making me catch my breath.

Once at the car, he releases my hand and opens the door for me.

I stop, standing in front of the open door. "That was awesome," I tell him.

"It was," he agrees. "I'm not sure if I should hug you or throttle you."

"I vote for hug."

"I don't think you get to vote."

I pretend pout and he shakes his head, laughing softly and looking down at his feet.

"I'm still going to get you back," he says.

"I look forward to it," I say, and then I slide in the car.

21

It is important for all of us to appreciate where we come from and how that history has really shaped us in ways that we might not understand.

—Sonia Sotomayor

Dean

After leaving the fair, we drive in silence for a while. I think Freya is starting to fall asleep, but I can't hold it in any longer. I have to find a way to get her to tell me what happened with her and that goddamn asshole. I know he did something to her, and I think if I can get her to open up about it...I don't know, maybe I can help her somehow, the way she's helped me.

And I don't mean just with the murder charge. I mean, she's helped me come alive, when I didn't even realize that I've been barely living for years.

"You never told me," I say loudly and she jerks upright in the seat next to me. I feel a momentary pang of guilt for intentionally waking her up, but I'm pretty tired too and if she falls asleep, I might join her. Which would be bad since I'm driving.

"Never told you what?" she asks.

"You were supposed to tell me about Cooper, after I told you what happened with Angelica."

For a moment I think she considers it. She's silent but then something shudders through her and she says, "I can't talk about it yet."

"Fine," I say abruptly. "Let's make a bet."

"What kind of bet?"

"The stakes are this: if I win, you tell me what happened. If you win, you don't have to tell me anything. Unless you want to."

"Okay," she says slowly, seemingly surprised at my suggestion. "And what are the terms?"

"Whoever initiates the next kiss loses."

She laughs. "What?"

"You heard me. If you kiss me, you lose. If I kiss you first, I lose."

"That's the most ridiculous bet ever."

"Is it? We seem to have the tendency to make out with each other, and you are usually ridiculous."

"Can't argue with the truth. What kind of kiss are we talking about?" she asks.

"On the mouth," I say quickly. "A kiss on the cheek or anywhere else doesn't count."

She's quiet as she mulls it over. The way I see it, this is a win-win situation. I have the opportunity to drive her crazy, and either she kisses me and I win, or I kiss her, and well... even if I lose, I've already won.

"Fine," she says. "You're on." She sticks her hand out and I reach over to give her a quick shake.

"Okay then," I say, glad that's settled. "Now, tell me a story or something. I didn't sleep much last night and I don't want to fall asleep at the wheel."

"What do you want to know about?" she asks.

"Tell me about your mom. You told her I was coming with you, right?"

She waves the question away. "She's cool."

I hope that's a yes.

"You said she's kind of a hippie? And a vegan? What else."

"I dunno, she's my mom. She's...open. Funny." I see her shoulders shrug out of the corner of my eye. "You'll see."

"What about your dad?" I ask.

"I don't have one."

"It's kind of impossible for you to be sitting here without someone other than your mother donating a chromosome. Are they divorced or something?"

"No."

Silence. "Is he dead?" I finally ask.

"I don't know. I really don't have a dad."

"So he took off before you were born?"

"You could say that."

I frown and glance over at her. "Why are you being so vague?"

She sighs. "She went to a sperm bank." The words come out fast, like she's hoping I won't hear or understand the words if she says them quickly enough.

A beat of silence and then, *"What?"*

"Don't make me repeat it." She smacks me on the arm.

"She...why?"

"Some of the world's greatest unsolved mysteries involve why my mom does anything. She wanted a kid, she didn't want a man. Can you blame her?"

"Wow." I shake my head. That was not what I expected. I can't help but chuckle.

"Okay, just don't mention it when we get there," she says.

"Why would I do that?"

"I don't know, just forget I told you."

A few minutes later we stop to fill up the tank, use the bathrooms and get Slurpees. Once we're back in the car and on the road, she asks me, "What about your dad?"

"What about him?"

"Where is he?"

"Took off when I was still a baby. Sarah is my half-sister."

"Where's her dad?"

"He's a drug addict and alcoholic. Last we heard, he was out of rehab and living in Michigan."

"Oh."

"Yeah."

She takes a drink of her Slurpee.

I suppose it's only fair I tell her the whole truth. I can't expect her to open up to me if I don't return the favor.

"He would get violent," I say.

I feel her turn and look at me.

I keep my eyes focused out the front windshield and on the road. "I tried to convince my mom to leave him, and she was going to, but then she got cancer for the first time. The chemo was really draining. Most days, she couldn't even get out of bed. She couldn't leave him."

She doesn't say anything, just listens. I want to see her expression, but I don't want to see it, either. So I continue. "That's when I started taking karate. They offered a class at the community center just a few blocks from our house. I was ten, Sarah was just a baby. I knew I would have to protect her and my mom. It took me so long to get good." I shake my head. "Too long. But by the time I was sixteen, he couldn't get past me. That's when he left."

She says nothing.

"I hate violence of any kind," I say.

I know exactly what she's thinking, and I anticipate her next remark.

"But you make a living with it."

"I make a living from other people fighting. I'm just the guy that organizes the events and takes the bets. I don't fight unless I absolutely have to, and that's only happened a couple of times when other guys don't show up and I had no other options."

"No wonder you were such an ass the first time I met you."

That makes me smile. She's never been afraid to insult

me, and I'm glad my sob story doesn't totally freak her out. I take a deep breath and let it out slowly. Now for the hard truth. "I have to tell you something."

"Okay."

"Promise you won't get mad."

"I hate it when people say that. It's not a fair request when I have no idea what you're about to say. Like, what if you tell me you put sugar in my gas tank, or slept with my mom? Of course I'm going to be mad, no matter what I promise beforehand."

I frown. "Have many people told you that they've slept with your mom?"

"Just one guy I went to high school with."

I laugh. She must be kidding, but a quick glance shows me she's not laughing with me. "Seriously?" I ask.

"I don't kid about such things. Now tell me what you need to tell me before I assume the worst."

"Fine." I take one final glance over at her before looking back at the road. "I never really beat up Chester."

I don't look over, but I can feel her eyes boring a hole into the side of my head.

"What do you mean? Of course you did. I saw the bruises."

I shake my head. "No. When you told me who it was, I knew he would be fighting someone the next week and he's a shitty fighter, so I knew he would be bruised up. He owed me a debt and agreed to fight to pay it off. I never touched him."

"But you took my money!"

"Yeah."

"And you told me it was my fault all these girls starting hiring you!"

"Well, technically, that's still your fault. You did tell people that I beat him up for you, and they believed it and I started getting into that business because of you. But I never actually hurt anyone or beat anyone up."

"You owe me a hundred bucks." She crosses her arms over her chest and pouts in the direction of the passenger window.

It's cute, really.

"I'll pay you back," I say, trying to hide the amusement from my voice and failing.

"With interest," she says.

"Now you're pushing it."

"You lied to me!"

"You lied, too. You said you were my sister."

"Yeah, but I didn't lie to *you*. You knew I wasn't your sister."

"You damn near gave me a heart attack thinking Sarah had shown up at one of the fights."

She heaves out a frustrated breath. "Why didn't you ever tell me?"

"I didn't want to upset you."

"Then why tell me now?"

"It feels wrong now, keeping it from you. And I will pay you back."

"You better," she mumbles.

We drive for a moment in silence and then I say, "You shouldn't be too mad. I didn't sleep with your mother."

"You do have that going for you," she concedes.

"And I would never put sugar in your gas tank. That piece of crap car has enough problems."

"Hey, hey, hey no talking crap about Fiona."

"Fiona? You named your car after a Shrek character?"

"Exactly. She's green. And she's a princess and an ogre."

"Sort of like you."

This makes her laugh, and I know I'm forgiven. "Now you're catching on."

22

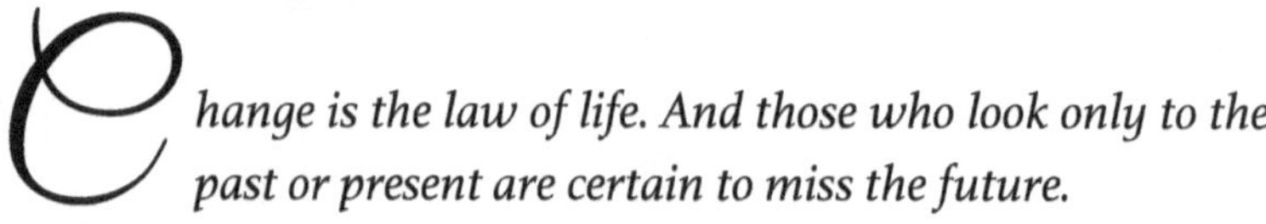

Change is the law of life. And those who look only to the past or present are certain to miss the future.

—John F. Kennedy

Freya

I am totally going to win this whole bet thing Dean started. It's too easy. I don't have to work at not kissing someone. He's going to lose for sure—he's the guy.

I still can't believe what he told me about his stepdad. I sort of suspected something from his comments and what his mom had said, but it's different hearing the words spoken out loud and not having just a vague thought in my mind.

It's hard not to tell him my story, after he shared his. For the rest of the drive I consider opening my mouth, saying the words, telling him what happened, but something inside me shudders. The way I see it, this could go a couple of ways. I tell him, he thinks I'm lying or exaggerating or worse, that I deserved it because I was leading Cameron on. Let's face it, we were together when it happened. Or, I tell him and he sees me the way I see me. Damaged. Ruined. Dirty. Broken.

Before I have a chance to open my mouth and spill, we're pulling into town. We made it just before dinner time.

"My mom's probably still at the shop. We'll have to go there to pick up the keys," I tell Dean when we've crossed into city limits.

"Okay."

I direct him onto the main road. It's an old-fashioned street, lined with newly blooming trees and shops on either side.

He parks down the street and then we walk to the store.

My mom's place is a vegan sandwich slash bohemian accoutrement shop. One side is the deli, and the other side is full of hippie clothes, and vintage furniture (and the odd glass pipe here and there).

It's called *Psychadelicatessen*.

A tinkling bell announces our presence when I push open the door.

There's a couple in line at the deli, and I can see my mom behind the counter putting together some food.

She glances up when the bell rings and when she sees

me her eyes light up. "Hey! You made it! And you brought a friend?"

I feel Dean tense beside me. "You didn't tell her?" he whispers out of the corner of his mouth.

"It's easier this way. Just follow my lead," I murmur back before taking his hand and leading him over to the register.

We wait while her customers pay and then she washes her hands and steps out from behind the counter to greet us.

She gives me a hug before stepping back and looking Dean up and down.

"Dean, this is my mom, Jane. Mom, this is Dean," I say. I can see the thoughts forming in her eyes and I know she's going to ask some horrible, humiliating question, so I say the only thing that will cause the least amount of interrogation. "He's my boyfriend."

I immediately feel Dean's eyes boring a hole into the side of my head.

"Oh," my mom says. "Well, you could have done worse." She looks over to Dean. "You're a total hunk."

"Mom!"

"What? It's the truth. You want the keys? I'm locking up now and I'll bring some sandwiches home. You like falafel, Dean?"

"Sure." He looks a little shell shocked.

"Of course you do, you're a sweet boy." She pats him on the cheek before turning away to get the keys.

I grab the keys from her and then we head back to his car.

While we're buckling up, he asks, "Boyfriend?"

"I didn't want to tell her about the whole murder-suspect-shooting thing. She'll freak. This is much easier to explain. Fewer invasive questions. Less worrying and hand wringing and rending of the hair."

He pulls into traffic and tosses me a quick glance before shaking his head.

"You could've said we're friends."

I wonder for a second if that's what we are. Are we friends?

"Then I'd have to deal with her trying to hook us up all week. This is much easier."

He tosses me an odd glance. "Your mom would try to hook us up? Really?"

"Or she might try to sleep with you. You have no idea."

"You could have warned me or told me what the story was going to be before I met her."

"I didn't think you would go along with it."

"You thought a surprise attack was the best way to go?"

I can't help but grin at him. "With you, it usually is."

"That's fine," he says. "Boyfriend is good. It will give you more of an opportunity to kiss me."

I laugh. "I'm so not going to kiss you."

"We'll see about that," he murmurs.

I direct him towards the house and a few minutes later, we're pulling up the long gravel drive. The house I grew up in is a small, two-bedroom wooden structure that Mom has slowly turned sustainable over the years. There's solar panel rooftop shingles, flowers in pots adorning the entryway, and the entire house is surrounded by plants—a mishmashed garden of herbs, fruits and vegetables.

By the time we've dragged our suitcases up to the small porch, my mom comes tearing up the drive after us.

We've barely made it into the small, tiled entryway when she's opening the door behind us.

"Let me just put dinner in the fridge and then I'll show you kiddos to your room," she says before heading into the kitchen.

"I know where my room is," I call to her retreating back, but she's not listening to me.

"Room?" Dean asks me. "Doesn't she mean rooms?"

"We only have two bedrooms, hers and my old room."

"But—"

"Come on then!" My mom is back, a whirling dervish of red curls and patchouli scent.

I shrug at Dean and we follow her down the narrow hallway.

"Here we are!" She opens the door with a flourish.

Right after I moved out, she changed the entire room, took down all of my old high school photo collages, boy band posters, and repainted the bright pink walls (I picked the color when I was ten) to a more sophisticated pale green.

"Um, I can sleep on the couch," Dean says.

"Nonsense." My mom waves away the suggestion. "No reason for you to be sneaking around on my behalf. I wasn't born yesterday."

I toss my bag onto the neatly made bed and turn back

in time to see Dean's alarmed expression. I bite my lip to avoid laughing.

"And there's a vase on the mantle in the living room that's completely filled with condoms, so if you're going to have sex, make sure you're safe, okay pumpkins?"

"Mom!" I say, too loudly in the small space.

"What? I'm old, I'm not dead. Don't use too many of those condoms, I might need some for myself." Then she winks at Dean. "I'll meet you in the dining room once you've settled in."

And with that little pronouncement, she leaves.

Dean's face is absolutely stricken. "Did she just...did I imagine that entire conversation?"

"You can try to pretend it didn't happen, but years of therapy won't erase it from your mind."

"Your mom." He enters the room and tosses his bag on the bed next to mine. "She just gave me permission to take advantage of you. In her home."

"Yep."

"You really weren't kidding about her sleeping with someone you went to school with?"

"Nope."

"Is she nuts?"

"Nah, just very open. Don't worry about it, we've slept in the same bed before. I promise, your virtue is safe with me. But if you're still concerned, you can sleep on the floor."

He glances down at the dark hardwood floors before sighing and flopping onto his back on the bed, staring up towards the slowly rotating ceiling fan. "It makes sense now," he says.

"What makes sense now?" I ask. I open my suitcase and pull out my plastic case of bathroom items. I walk over to the opposite doorway, putting it on the counter in the small attached bath.

"You. You're nuts, too. It's genetic."

I consider that. "Probably."

I walk back to the bed and plop down on my back next to him, legs swinging over the side.

"Is there anything else I should be prepared for before we go out there and eat dinner?"

"Nope," I say, staring at the leaf-shaped ceiling fan above my head.

I hear him shift and turn towards me. "You wouldn't tell me if there was, would you?"

I look over at him. He's propped his head on his hand, blue eyes focused down on me.

"Nope," I say.

He leans towards me suddenly, moving so close I can feel his breath on my lips.

My breath hitches in my throat.

A penny couldn't fit in the space between our mouths.

His lips hover over mine for a millisecond before he dips his head down and brushes his mouth against my neck, initiating a rush of tingles that spread in a throbbing path down my body.

Almost immediately, he pulls himself up to standing, clapping his hands, like none of that just happened, "Well. Let's go then, girlfriend."

"So, Dean, what's your major?" My mom asks once we're seated around the small circular dining table.

"Molecular Biology," he says. "I eventually want to be an oncologist."

I nearly choke on my falafel. How did I not know this? "Really?" I ask.

My mom smacks her hand on the table. "You don't know his major?" she asks me. "What kind of girlfriend are you? No, wait, don't answer because I already know you're spending too much time blabbing about yourself and you're not listening to anything else."

"Mom!"

"What? You think I don't know my own daughter?" She turns to Dean, who I can see is smiling and enjoying my own personal humiliation, as usual. "She's always been like this," she says to him. "When she was a little girl, she would always boss around her friends and try to get them into her little schemes until they didn't want to play with her anymore."

"Do we really have to talk about this?"

"It's the truth!"

"Schemes?" Dean asks.

"Oh yes, she decided one day that poor Mickey who runs the animal control center was abusing the animals and she convinced one of her friends to help her sneak in and set them all free." She makes a tsking sound. "Took poor Mickey and the shelter volunteers two days to round all of them up again."

"Well, they were keeping them in little cages," I attempt to defend myself.

"It's a no-kill shelter. Those animals would die out in the woods on their own."

"I was six! I didn't understand those things."

She pats me on the hand. "You've always been a lover. Animal lover, people lover. Always wanting to help others. It's why your name is so fitting."

"Her name?" Dean asks.

"Freya. The Norse goddess of love," Mom tells him.

"Ah."

"She's also associated with war and death," I add.

"Now that makes sense," Dean says with a grin.

"Ha, ha, very funny." I stick out my tongue at him.

"I think you guys are a good match," Mom says suddenly.

"Really?" Dean asks.

"You both have an innate need to help others. A doctor and a lawyer." She smacks the table again and smiles at us. "I think it's kismet."

I meet Dean's eyes across the table and have to look away, feeling a moment of embarrassment and guilt. I should tell her the truth.

"Anyone want dessert? I made cupcakes!" Mom says, getting up to clear the table.

Vegan cupcakes, I mouth at Dean behind her back and then I make a puke face.

He ignores me.

"Do you need help?" Dean asks, starting to stand.

"Of course not, you sweet boy. You guys just relax, I

know how exhausting being in the car all day can be." She pats his hand before disappearing into the kitchen.

"She is kinda crazy, but she's nice," Dean says once she's out of earshot. I hear water running, the clatter of dishes, and her singing. He looks around the cluttered and eclectic dining room and leans back a little in his seat. "I like it here."

Our eyes meet again. Dean's smiling and I can't look away. His eyes look lighter. They're always the same blue, but for some reason they normally seem darker, deeper... more troubled. Right now, they're bright, as if a light is shining from behind them.

We stare at each other for a few long moments and tension seeps into the space between us, wrapping its tingling fingers around my body. The table is small and his knee brushes mine. My eyes are drawn from his eyes to his lips.

I'm not sure I can handle it. I have to say something to cut the taut wire of awareness that's compelling me towards him like a tractor beam.

"You look different," I say.

"I do?"

"Yeah. You look relaxed. Not as tense as you usually are. You're not frowning or bossing me around or anything. It's a good look for you."

He laughs. "Maybe it's because we're off the grid."

I nod. It's almost a relief to have no cell service. Don't have to worry about anyone finding us or shooting at us. We're not trying to solve a mystery, and it feels good.

I'm about to say something embarrassing about how I

have free reign to take advantage of him, but I'm interrupted by my mom's voice escalating.

Dean's expression shifts and he looks perturbed.

"What is she singing?"

I focus on the words and then sigh. "NWA."

"The rap group? The totally inappropriate, full-of-expletives, parental-advisory-included, rap group?"

"Yeah. She's got a real thing for Ice Cube."

He laughs. "No way."

"Yes way."

We laugh and the tension shifts away, hovering around the edges while we make small talk. Mom comes back out with her cupcakes and we eat and drink chamomile tea and play gin rummy until bedtime.

When I lose the last hand, I leave them to finish the game and go into my old room to get ready for bed.

I wash my face and I'm working on brushing my teeth when I hear the door to the bedroom open and close. I spit my toothpaste into the sink, run the water, and then stick my head out the door in time to see Dean pulling his shirt over his head.

Dang it, why am I constantly being barraged with his naked body? This is ridiculous! He's doing it on purpose. He wants me to crack and make out with him. But I'm not going to let it affect me.

I sneak another peek around the open doorway and this time he's fully clothed and facing my direction.

"Oh, hey," I say, surprised to be caught in the act.

He smiles like he knows exactly what I'm thinking and I yank my head back into the bathroom.

"I'm almost done," I call out.

"No worries," he calls back. I hear the shifting of the mattress like he's sitting on the bed.

I quickly finish, cleaning up my mess before heading into the bedroom. The room is fairly dark, just one small lamp on a side table setting a soft glow over everything.

Dean's lying back on the bed with his arms behind his head, eyes closed. At some point, he also changed his pants from jeans to flannel PJ bottoms. How did I miss that show?

I step to his side of the bed and clear my throat. He opens his eyes and looks at me.

"The bathroom's all yours," I say.

"Thanks," he says. He doesn't move. The awareness between us that never really left starts building again.

He rolls to his feet suddenly, getting too close, and I instinctively move back, running into the dresser.

He steps closer, putting his arms on either side of my body, resting his hands on the furniture behind me. I have nowhere to go. His face is right in front of mine. This is it. He's going to kiss me. I know it. I can practically feel it already. His hands will be everywhere, sliding all over my body, he'll rip my clothes off, and then we'll take his clothes off—

My daydream is interrupted when he reaches a hand up, cupping it against my cheek. His thumb moves against the corner of my mouth. "You have a little toothpaste, here," he whispers.

The warmth disappears from my face and he's gone, the bathroom door shutting gently behind him.

"Toothpaste?" I mutter. "Toothpaste! Goddamn him."

"Did you say something?" The words are muffled from behind the door.

"Nope. Nothing!"

I pull my suitcase out from under the bed and start rifling through the clothes I brought. Two can play this game.

23

Law is reason free from passion.

–Aristotle

**ean**

I brush my teeth in record time. Anxious to return to Freya and continue driving her slowly mad with lust. This is the most fun I've had...ever.

When I step out of the bathroom, the lamp is still on, casting a soft glow over the bed and Freya.

She's lying with her back to me and she's wearing...holy hell, almost nothing. A flimsy little pink tank top and a pair of matching barely-there shorts.

I stop next to the bed, the opposite side of where she's lying, and take off my shirt, letting it plop to the ground.

I know she hears me because she tenses slightly.

I don't move, choosing to wait her out. I have the advantage because I can see her, but she can't see me.

It doesn't take long. Less than a minute passes in silence before she rolls over and looks up at me, her gaze travelling over my body.

"It's really not fair," she says.

"What's not fair?" I ask, and my brain short circuits for a moment when I see her from the front. That top really is flimsy.

"You." She gestures towards me. "You're so much hotter than I am. There's no way I can win our bet."

It takes me a moment to register her words. I'm too busy imagining what she looks like under the clothes, and what I want to do to her right now, but once they hit my foggy brain I propel myself into the bed next to her, as close as I can get, and run a hand down her arm.

"That's ridiculous," I say forcefully, willing her to believe it.

"Not ridiculous."

"What do I have to do to prove to you that you're beautiful?" I ask.

She blinds me with a smile. "Kiss me."

I smile back, and for a split second, I want to comply. My mouth finds its own trajectory towards hers, but I remember the big picture at the last minute and instead brush my lips across her jaw. I move down her neck and over to her ear where I tug the lobe gently between my teeth.

"Oh, God," she whispers.

"You're always getting my name wrong," I mutter against her neck.

That makes her giggle. "Oh, Mob guy," she says.

"If you're laughing, I'm doing something wrong. And you know I hate that moniker."

"Oh, Thor."

I lift my head to look down at her. "You really think that's better?" And then I dig my fingers into her sides, tickling her and making her jerk and squeak and laugh. I'm really enjoying the movement of her body as it shakes with laughter, but after a minute, when she starts trying to kick me in the head, I give her a break and rest my head on her stomach.

We're quiet for a moment, catching our breath, and I start thinking about everything we did today.

"I really like your mom," I say.

"Aaand my libido just tanked."

I lift my head to smile at her. "I'm serious. I feel bad lying to her."

"Well, you don't have to say anything. I'll do the lying for you, so your conscience is clear."

"Actually, I was thinking..." I have to look away. I sit up so we are no longer touching. I'm nervous about how she's going to take what I have to say next. I'm pretty sure we're on the same page, but I have to know for sure.

"A dangerous pastime," she says, trying to lighten the

nervous tension that seems to have suddenly filled the small space.

I smile and try to figure out the best way to put what's in my head into words. "I was thinking, maybe we don't have to lie to her."

"What do you mean?" she asks, sitting up next to me.

"Come on," I say. "You have to have thought about it, at some point in the last month. We've spent a lot of time together, we get along—most of the time—we keep making out...there's something here." I gesture into the space between us.

She says nothing, just stares at me, expression blank and I start to sweat.

But then, she leans towards me, pausing for just a moment when our lips are only a hairsbreadth apart. I intake a sharp puff of breath and then her mouth is pressing against mine.

I'm not sure what to do, or what this means. The kiss is soft and gentle, and I keep it that way even though my body is screaming to take it further, letting her have all of the control. But after a minute I have to touch her. I gently run my fingertips along her jaw and chin.

She pulls away and looks at me.

"What does that mean?" I ask.

She flops back onto her back, staring up at the ceiling.

"It means I concede. You win the bet." She tilts her head to look up at me. "I'm going to tell you everything, and then you may or may not wish to change your mind about being my—"

She stops suddenly and a look of panic flashes over her

face. She sits up on her elbows and meets my eyes. "Wait, you're saying you want us to be, like, together right? Boyfriend and girlfriend? Please tell me I didn't misinterpret your whole spiel just now, because that's totally something I would do." She bites her lip.

I take her hand and link it with mine, shifting a little closer to her on the bed. "Yes, that's what I meant," I say. "I've never met anyone quite like you, Freya. You never let anyone or anything scare you. You don't judge. You're funny and smart and you put up with a lot of my shit and yet you still want to help me. You continually take me by surprise. Plus, you're pretty hot."

She flushes at the compliments and looks away.

"You're not so bad yourself," she says with a small smile.

I bring her fingers to my mouth and kiss her knuckles lightly.

"Okay." She breathes out a sigh and flops back onto the bed, her hand still entwined with mine, her gaze on the ceiling. "I'm not really sure where to start."

"Take your time. Start at the beginning," I suggest.

She takes a deep breath and lets it out slowly, shutting her eyes before she speaks. "I met Cameron the first week of junior year. The first two years of college, I stayed here and went to a nearby community college. I've always lived here, so when I transferred, I was the typical stupid girl, going to college in the big city—well bigger city—just a small town girl."

"Living in a lonely world?"

She laughs. "Totally. And Cameron was...charming. Worldly. One of those people that when they talk to you, it's like you're the only person in the room. He made me feel important, valued, cherished. I didn't date much in high school. Despite my wild mom, I was a late bloomer when it came to guys. I just never met anyone that made me feel...anything. So when I met Cameron and I started having feelings for him, it was so new and exciting. When he started to pull away, it only made me want to hold on to those feelings even harder. It was weird. He was still super sweet to me when we were alone, or when it suited him, I guess. But when other people were around or whatever, he would practically ignore me and like the dumbass I was, I let him do it. It just made me work harder to gain his attention."

She stops and takes another breath before continuing. "He had been pressuring me for sex, and I wasn't sure I was ready. I was a virgin. I know, it's weird right?" She doesn't give me a chance to answer, and she's still got her eyes shut. "So, when he started to withdraw, I gave that to him, thinking it would fix everything. But instead of it bringing us closer, he pulled farther away.

"I hate this part, because it's where I start to do things even stupider than losing my virginity to an asshole. So, one day class was cancelled and I went to his dorm, knowing he would be free. Instead I caught him banging Liz the slut. That was it, I thought. That was the push I needed to forget about him and move on with my life. I was hurt, frustrated, everything made me cry. It was pathetic. That's when I got the idea to take some control back and have someone pummel the living shit out of him."

"That's when you came to me," I say, squeezing her hand gently.

"Yeah," she scoffs. She opens her eyes and tilts her head towards mine. "Making one bad decision after another."

"Well, I'm glad for that bad decision now. At the time, I was pretty ticked."

"You were. Grumpy pants."

"The night we met, one of the guys who was supposed to fight pulled out at the last second and I had no one to step in. I hate fighting. Being in charge of the bets is bad enough."

"I'm glad you were there," she says. "Even though I wasn't so sure at the time." She smiles at me and then she averts her gaze again, her eyes moving around the room and back up to the ceiling. "After *someone else* beat him up." She tries to flash me a sideways glare, but it's about as effective as an angry puppy, before she continues. "I did the dumbest thing yet. I got back together with him."

This is new information for me. "You got back together with that asshole?"

"Yes. I know, I realize now it was stupid, but unfortunately as much as I wish a loud booming voice had echoed through the sky BAD DECISION FREYA that has yet to happen. Although it would have been useful on more than one occasion. He came crawling back and begging for forgiveness, promising he would change, it would be different, I would change him and you know, what dumb girl doesn't want to hear that? And it was okay, for a while. Even better than it was when we first met. But, I told him, I didn't want to have sex with him. We fooled around still, a little, but I didn't want to take that step until I was sure I could completely trust him. He seemed to understand, and things went along for a couple of weeks.

"Then, one night, we were fooling around..." she breaks off and looks over at me. I stare back, waiting. I almost want to stop her. I'm not sure I can handle hearing it—even though I'm not one-hundred percent sure what *it* is—without wanting to kill the asshole. All I know is he hurt her somehow, and even though I'm not sure I can take it, I need to take it for Freya. She needs to get this out of her, it's the only way to move forward.

"This is the hardest part. I've never shared the details with anyone—only Lucy knows the highlights—but I need to share them with you. You need to know how broken I am before you decide to tie yourself to me."

I agree that she needs to share it, but I don't agree with the broken part and at this point, there isn't anything in this world that could prevent me from tying myself to her. I want to tell her this, but I don't want to get her off track and I don't want to totally freak her out. We aren't even officially together yet, so I just nod and squeeze her hand again, saying nothing.

"We were fooling around," she says. "Just making out and stuff, and he started popping the button on my jeans. I told him no, moved his hands away, and we went back to just kissing. But then he did it again. This time, I didn't say anything. Within minutes, my pants were off. But we just kept kissing, nothing more. A little while later, I realized his pants were off, too, and that's when I tried to put a stop to it, but then he was on top of me."

She stops for a second, her breath coming out a little faster. "I said no, I tried to push him away, but he just yanked my underwear to the side and pushed himself inside me. I didn't know what to do. I was kind of shocked when it happened, and it was like it wasn't happening to me but to someone else. We were in his dorm, and his roommate had this poster—one of those motivational posters with a waterfall and some lame saying—and all I could do was stare at it and pretend like I was somewhere else. Afterwards, he acted like nothing had happened. No big deal. When I tried to bring it up the next day, he got super defensive and said if I thought he was a rapist then maybe we shouldn't be together. He was using that as a way to control me, threatening to break up, thinking that would be enough to make me forget about it and stay with him. It almost worked. He stopped returning my calls, and I heard he was seeing someone else. But instead of being upset, all I felt was relief. He tried to talk to me and chat me up a few weeks later when I ran into him, but by then I was completely over it." She shakes her head at the memory. "I told him to fuck off. He was shocked, like no one had ever rejected him before."

She gives me a hesitant glance. This whole time, she didn't look at me once which is probably a good thing because I can feel my jaw clenching to hold back the pissed-off words wanting to get out. I suddenly realize that I've got her hand in a vice grip.

She tries to remove her hand from mine—I feel the small tug, but I'm not ready to let her go yet.

"What are you thinking?" she asks after a moment.

I need to answer her, but first I need to move. I stand up and start pacing the floor in front of the bed. "I'm thinking I'm going to fucking kill that bastard."

"That might defeat the whole thing where we're trying to exonerate you of murder."

"I don't care. I want to rip his balls off and feed them to him."

"Dean." She stands and moves in front of me, halting my frantic pacing. "It's okay, it's over now. I'm...getting over it. But you need to know about it, because I'm a bit damaged. I've been trying to fix it. I thought that maybe, if I could find someone else who was exactly opposite of everything Cameron was and sleep with him a million times—"

"What?!" Is she kidding me?

"No, wait, just listen. I was wrong. I didn't sleep with anyone else. I can't because I flinch or freak out—as you've noticed—whenever anyone gets too close to me. It's like I can barely stand to be touched anymore."

As a counterpoint to her words, I reach out and grab her, pulling her into a tight embrace. "You thought that fucking someone else would help?" My voice comes out harsher than I intend, so I kiss the top of her head. I feel better with her in my arms. Nothing can hurt her as long as I'm with her.

"I thought it would help me feel in control again," she says against my chest. "The fact that I can't let anyone touch me is giving Cameron more power than he should have. It's like he still controls me even though we aren't together anymore. I want the power back. I want my life back."

"You're not flinching now."

"No."

"I could be this guy you sleep with a million times," I say into her hair, only half kidding.

She leans her head back to look up at me. "You could. But even with you, when we start moving too fast I just panic. Plus, you have enough people to take care of. I don't want you to feel like you have to take care of me, too."

Is she serious? "Have you met you? You don't need to be taken care of. You tend to take matters into your own hands, for better or worse."

"I know but, I don't think you know what you're getting yourself into. I might not be ready for a long time."

"Ready for what?"

"You know...intimacy."

My eyebrows lift and I rub her shoulders gently. "You think I care about that?"

"Don't most guys care about that?"

"Fuck those guys! Wait, no, don't fuck those guys," I quickly retract.

She rolls her eyes but then a laugh escapes.

"Seriously, Freya. I can wait. I'm willing to stay here, and be whatever you need, do whatever you need. I'm in no hurry. Besides." I give her my best grin. "Sometimes the anticipation makes it that much better."

"You're sure?"

"Yes. I can sleep with you without molesting you."

"Isn't that really hard?" she asks.

I smirk. "It might be really *hard*."

She smacks me on the arm. "You know what I mean."

"I do. And no, it's not that *difficult*. I'm a man, not an animal."

"There's a difference?"

"Yes. Opposable thumbs." But then I remember that I don't have much to offer. And I come with more than just emotional scars. I have a whole family of problems. "Are you sure you want to be with *me*? I come with baggage too, you know. I'm not always as charming as you are. I have a hard time being nice to anyone when I'm stressed and worried about my family."

"I hide all my feelings and you can't hide shit," she says with a laugh.

"Does that bother you?"

"Nah. Grumpy looks good on you."

I have to smile at that, and then I take her hand, interlacing our fingers. "Isn't that weird? It's almost like our imperfections make us perfect for each other."

Her mouth drops open slightly at my words, and I worry for a second that I've said too much. I shake my head at myself and tug gently on her hand. "Come on. Let's get some sleep."

I get under the covers and slide to the far side, not letting go of her hand until she's scooted in beside me. I pull her against me and she rests her head on my bicep, our legs flush together.

I rub her back, hoping that eventually she'll be so used to my touch I'll drive her demons away. Or maybe she needs to be completely in control, with me unable to touch her at all. I whisper into the darkness, "Would it help if you tied me up and I couldn't touch you?"

"What? No! This isn't *Fifty Shades of Gray*, buddy."

I laugh. "There she is! I was a little worried because you haven't cracked a joke or said something sarcastic in like an hour. I think that's some kind of record."

She punches me lightly in the arm, but laughs out loud.

I pull her even closer and kiss her mouth, trying to catch her laughter.

She kisses me back and then snuggles into me, and I realize I've never been as content as I am right at this moment.

"Good night," I whisper into her hair.

"Good night."

24

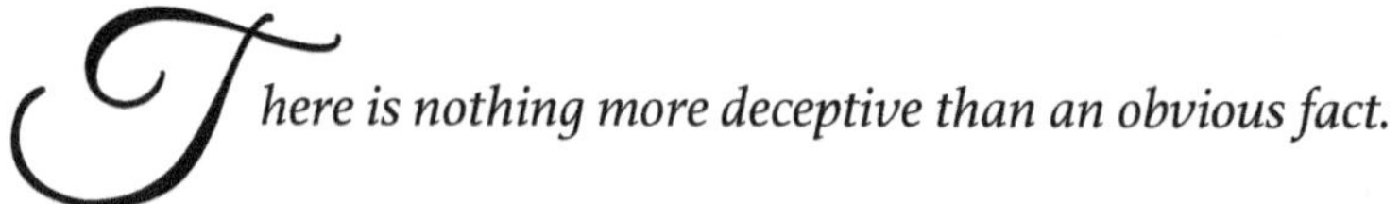

There is nothing more deceptive than an obvious fact.

–Arthur Conan Doyle

Freya

We spend the next few days in this weird, content universe. Hanging out with my mom, going on hikes, splashing around in the river even though it's still freezing cold, working in the garden and drinking tea. It's almost like the last month hasn't happened.

And Dean is my boyfriend. For reals. I have no idea how to react to this. I haven't even thought the word *boyfriend* at any point in the last six months. All I've thought is "friend with benefits" and "dear Lord let me be okay with a guy touching me without flailing like a moron."

I'm not sure I can handle a relationship. I'm still not sure I'm any good for anyone, even after our talk the other night.

I keep thinking about the things he's done for his mom and his sister. Despite his own personal inclinations against violence, he found a way to help his family and do whatever it takes to keep them fed and happy. And I'm...well, me.

And while I'm not one of those girls who's gonna be like, *oh, no, he's too good for me,* and start simpering all over the place like I didn't just win the boyfriend lottery. I have to admit, I do care about him. I only want what's best for him, and what if I'm not what's best for him? Sure, I'm not bad, but maybe he could be with someone better. Someone smarter. Hotter. With bigger boobs, a smaller nose, and fewer personal issues. He's been through enough shit without adding mine to the pile.

But I told him everything, and he made his decision. He still wants me, as broken and battered as I am, and I don't think I could let him go at this point even if I really wanted to.

The day before we're going to head back to school, the phone rings.

"It's Lucy!" Mom calls from the open doorway.

Dean and I are sitting on a bench swing on the front porch. I'm trying to convince him to let me drive on the way home and he's arguing that he can't put the public at such a risk while he massages my feet.

He's totally winning that argument.

I reluctantly pull my feet from his lap and head inside.

"Hey Luce! What's shaking my little muffin top?" I sit on the chair next to the phone and play with the cord. My mom has an old rotary phone. To dial a number, you have to stick your finger in a hole with the number marked in it and drag it around a circle. It's so weird. I wonder how people survived before cell phones. I mean, if your house was on fire, you would burn to death before you could dial anything.

"I found some interesting information. It changes everything," she says.

"What is it?"

"I don't know how to tell you this," Lucy says and my stomach plummets. Did she find more evidence that incriminates Dean? I'm sure he didn't do it, but this can't be good.

"Dude, you're killing me smalls. Out with it!"

"Cameron," she says quickly.

"What?"

"Daisy's brother sold a nine-millimeter caliber gun, the same type of gun used to kill Jesse and Matt, to Cameron."

It takes a second for her words to sink in.

"When?"

"I don't know yet. It was posted for sale on a website before Jesse's murder, and there's no indication anywhere of where or when the actual transaction took place."

"Is that legal? Don't they have to register the sale or something?"

"No. According to federal gun laws, a person is allowed

to buy or sell a firearm from an unlicensed resident of their state if they do not have reasonable cause to believe the person is prohibited from owning guns."

"Why would Cameron kill Jesse and Matt? Do you think he's working with Daisy? And why? I don't know, Lucy..."

"I'm not sure. I'm still researching to find any more information that will make the rest of it make sense. Think about it. We'll talk again when you guys get back."

And with that, she hangs up.

After a second, I put the phone back in its nook and walk out to the porch.

"So?" Dean asks.

"She found some evidence that links Cameron to the crimes," I say, wrinkling my nose. I repeat what she told me on the phone.

"Huh." He eyes me sidelong. "You think she's wrong?"

I shake my head. "He's too obvious a suspect."

"What do you mean?"

"Don't you know how these things work? When there's a mystery to be solved, it's always the person you least suspect, not the person you hope it is."

He laughs. "This isn't an Agatha Christie novel."

"You're right," I sigh and sit down on the swing next to him. "If this was an Agatha Christie novel, the writing would be way better."

He takes my hand, kissing my wrist before putting our hands in his lap. "So, what should we do now? We have to find a way to eliminate or confirm Clinton as the murderer. And where does Daisy fit into all of this? Is she connected, or was suspecting her of the crime just wishful thinking on our part?"

Hmmm. I tap a finger against my chin for a few seconds. A bird chirps in the distance, the sound melting into the hum of crickets.

"Well, we could tap me with a wire, then I could invite him over and trick a confession out of him."

Dean shakes his head at me. "You have a death wish or something. You're always rushing headlong into danger and putting yourself in crazy situations. Hey, remember when I caught you sneaking around in the bushes that one day? What was that all about?"

"Bushes?"

"Yeah. Don't you remember? It was a few months ago, early December maybe? I was taking a shortcut through this alley to get to class, and you had your head stuck in a bush."

"Oh, right. I thought Jensen was cheating on Lucy, so I followed him home. I was spying on them."

He shakes his head. "You are the worst spy ever. That was funny though."

"I'm glad you derive amusement from my crazy, and that was not funny. You thought I was an idiot."

"I did not think you were an idiot."

"Well you acted like you thought I was an idiot."

"Maybe I was just nervous." He shrugs.

This takes me aback. "I don't believe that. You're never nervous."

"I'm human, it happens."

"Human? You mean, you're not the crown prince of

Asgard?" I ask in feigned shock.

He chuckles. "You make me nervous sometimes."

"Why?"

"I never know when you're going to come out of nowhere and hit me with your car."

I smack him on the arm and he laughs.

The next day, we leave Mom's. She sends us off with hugs and a cooler full of vegetables and tofu.

The drive home flies by in moments. It takes the normal eight hours, but my mind keeps whirring around one thing: I was wrong. I can't make someone else make me forget Cameron.

This whole time, I've been thinking if only I could let someone else touch me, if only I could change my last experience with intimacy and turn it into something else, then I could forget it ever happened, like a clean slate.

The problem with my grand plan is that I'm still letting other people control me. I'm putting the responsibility on others, when all along, the power to break Cameron's hold over me has been mine, and mine alone.

I have to face my demons myself. I can't rely on anyone to do it for me.

Opening up about the details to Dean was a good start. I hadn't told anyone that much. Hell, I hadn't even thought about it in that much detail since it happened, and now that it's out and Dean still wants me I feel...better.

He does make me feel better, even though I still realize that ultimately my healing will be up to me.

But just talking about it isn't good enough. There's only one other thing I can do to move on and confront my demons: I have to file charges. It's going to suck. No one wants to tell some stranger in a uniform who probably won't believe them about their sexual assault, but I suddenly feel like I have to. Even if it's my word against his —which it will be since it's been months and there's no evidence—but that doesn't change my mind. Dean was right. Even if nothing happens, maybe the next time Cameron decides to force himself on someone, her story will be believed if he has a documented history.

I agree to stay at Dean's place—not that he needed to do much convincing. I didn't want to be alone since there was still someone out there with malicious intents towards me. Or him, or both of us. Plus, his apartment is more heavily guarded and locked.

We're taking turns doing our laundry in the small, stackable machines in a closet next to the kitchen when I tell him.

"I'm going to file a police report about Cameron. For everything."

He stops transferring his clothes from the washer to the dryer and looks over at me. "Good," he says. Then he keeps doing laundry. "I'll come with you, if you want. Just let me know when."

"Okay."

"Are you hungry?"

"You know who you're asking, right?"

He shows me which drawer he keeps his takeout menus in, and I decide pho sounds really good, so we call in an order to the nearest Vietnamese restaurant.

"I'll go get it," Dean says, when a few minutes pass. "You stay here and relax." He pulls a bottle of red wine out of his cabinet.

"That's my favorite wine! How did you know?"

"Lucy." He gives me a shy smile.

"She is a genius."

He pours me a glass and leads me to the living room, pressing buttons before handing me the remote and the glass of wine. Something has already started on the TV.

My mouth drops open when I recognize the opening lines to *Love Actually*.

"And this is my favorite movie!"

He leans into me, kissing me hard and swift on the mouth before pulling back slightly. "I just want you to know that I care about you. A lot. And I would do anything to make you happy," he says. The words are simple, but his gaze is intense.

I can't do anything but stare. Is he for real?

He kisses me again and then he's moving towards the door.

"Engage all the locks behind me, okay?"

I can't find my tongue so I nod mutely.

He stands at the door, staring at me until I get up, and then he shuts the door behind him. But when I look through the peephole, he's waiting to hear me engage the dead bolt, the sliding metal door stopper, and the multitude of other turnkey type locks he's got on his door.

Once I've finished, I watch him leave through the peephole. He has such a nice ass. I hate to see him go, but I love to watch him leave.

I shuffle back to the couch.

What does he mean, practically telling me he loves me like that?

I reach for the wine, taking a big gulp while I try to concentrate on Bill Nighy attempting to sing "Christmas Is All Around."

Do I love Dean? My heart races and my stomach flips at the thought. I'm scared. Scared to open myself up to someone else. But Dean's so different from Cameron. Isn't he? Cameron never told me he cared about me like that. Hell, he never even told me he liked me. But he was also very good at pretending to be something that he wasn't. Dean's not like that. He's never pretended to be anything, as far as I know.

By the time Dean gets back with the food, I've barely touched the wine. I'm pacing back and forth, and Colin Firth has arrived at his cottage in France.

I check through the peephole before unlocking the chain and the rest of the locks and opening the door.

I take the food from him, putting it on the counter between the kitchen and living room while he's locking the door behind him.

When he turns around, I attack him.

Attack might be a strong word, but in this case I think it's fitting. I basically jump him—pulling his face down to mine because I'm too short to reach him—and kiss him with everything I've got.

It only takes him a second to respond after the initial shock of my assault and then he's lifting me up. I wrap my legs around his waist. He leans me against the wall, his hands holding me up under my thighs, still in the entryway, his hips rubbing into my center. I moan into his mouth.

He pulls back slightly, leaning his forehead against mine, breathing heavily, and says the one thing that might compel me to stop: "Our food's gonna get cold."

I shake my head slightly. "I don't care."

Weird, but true.

He pulls back farther at that, looking me in the eyes. "Are you sure?"

"Yes," I say before grabbing his head and pulling his mouth back to mine.

Kissing him is unlike anything I've ever experienced. I've kissed guys, sure, but not anyone I've felt anything for. Well, there was Cameron, but he doesn't count.

When I'm kissing Dean and he's kissing me...it's like a dance, a mutual sharing of affection and passion. I never want to stop. It makes me want to rip off all my clothes and burst into show tunes.

Dean's tongue is sliding against mine, and I feel like I could do this forever: kiss Dean against a wall. It gets intense and then suddenly he pulls back and gazes at me.

"What?" I say after a minute when I start to feel self-conscious from all the staring.

"Are you doing okay?"

"I'm fine. How are you?" I ask, a little confused about why he's asking for a moment, before I remember the last time we got hot and heavy and I had a super embarrassing panic attack. Oh, right. That.

Instead of responding, he just smiles and then hikes me up a little, pulling away from the wall before lifting me up and over his shoulder as easily as if I were a sack of dirt.

I squeal. I can't help it, I wasn't expecting him to toss me over his shoulder like that.

"*Now* are you taking me to your evil lair to have your wicked way with me?" I ask as he starts walking, jostling me slightly against him.

"Yes," he says and smacks me lightly on the butt. "If my evil lair is the couch." And with that, he tosses me onto the worn sofa, immediately following me down and hovering over me on the small space.

I expect him to go back to what we were doing before—getting all hot and bothered. But instead he moves slowly towards me until his lips move softly against mine, a light rubbing of lips, across and over, and over again. His hands run down my body, but not urgently. This time it's slow and soft. He kisses my nose, my eyelids, and then back to my mouth, barely touching his lips against mine.

"Tell me," he says against my mouth, "if you want me to stop."

"Don't stop," I whisper.

He kisses me again. He's being so gentle, touching me like I'm a bubble that might pop if handled too roughly.

It's great. Wonderful. Amazing. I've never felt so treasured in my life. Except after about five minutes of the light touches, I'm so turned on I think I might lose my mind. I try to get him to go faster, harder. I squeeze his biceps, running my hands up and down his back, under his T-shirt, putting my hands in his hair. When my ministrations don't entice him to take more action, I can't keep my mouth shut.

"If this is your wicked way, I think you're doing something wrong," I gasp.

His lips brush across my collarbone and down to where the top of my shirt meets skin.

"What do you mean?" he asks, his breath tickling me.

"I need..." I have no idea how to explain it. I have no experience with this. "I need *more*," I say finally.

"More what?" he asks, one of his hands moves lightly up my arm, pulling the strap of my top down before biting me gently.

"More everything!"

"I like driving you crazy," he says against my chest, right above my breasts where the fabric for the tank top begins. I can feel his smile against my skin.

I fist my hands in his hair and pull his head up to look him in the eyes. "Less foreplay, more action," I tell him.

He laughs then, and kisses me hard on the mouth. "As you wish," he whispers against my lips.

Then he's moving, running his nose along my jaw to kiss down my collar bone, sliding fabric away as he moves. I'm moving too, pulling at his T-shirt. He stops for a second and pulls it over his head and I try to admire his body up close, but he doesn't give me the time.

The next thing I know, my bra is unhooked and my top is pulled over my head and tossed somewhere on the ground. He's worshipping my body with his mouth. My legs have flopped open and he's lying in between them. I'm not really sure what to do with myself. The sensations coursing through me wherever his lips meet flesh are overwhelming, but not panic inducing. He makes his way down, pausing just above my pants, running his finger underneath the waistline, against my lower stomach.

He stops suddenly and rests his cheek against my belly. "We're not going to have sex tonight," he says, gazing up at me.

"What?" I can't comprehend the words coming out of his mouth. "What do you mean, no sex? You're going to deny me now?" My voice comes out way whinier than I intend.

He laughs against the sensitive skin of my lower stomach and I squirm against him.

"I'm not denying you anything," he says. "We just aren't having sex. Not tonight."

"Why not?"

"It's too soon."

"Too soon my ass!"

"Freya," he says, holding back laughter. "You've been through a lot. You might think you're ready now, and then you might regret it in the morning." His eyes meet mine, the normally bright blue color muted by the dim light. "I never want you to regret me."

I respond by reaching down and helping him slide all the clothes off my body and onto the floor. Surely, I can change his mind.

Before I have a chance to do or say anything else, his head is between my legs and his tongue is doing things that

I can't even fathom. I squirm underneath him, some of the sensations too intense, but he holds my hips steady with his hands. An embarrassingly short amount of time later, probably no more than two minutes, an orgasm rips through my body, making everything quake and tremble.

While I'm recovering, he kisses his way back up my body, settling beside me on the narrow couch and pulling me against him.

"You still have your pants on," I say against his chest.

"That's just self-preservation."

"You think I'm gonna go all nutso and chop off your balls while you sleep?"

"No." He pulls away slightly and kisses my forehead. "I don't want to be too tempted."

"To chop off your own balls while you sleep?"

He chuckles and sighs. "Hmm. Maybe."

After another moment, I pull away from him, stand up from the couch, and search for my clothes strewn all over the floor.

"What are you doing?" he asks.

"Well, since you aren't putting out, I'm going to get food. I need sustenance," I announce. I tug on my pants while scooting into the kitchen, grabbing the now too-cool-to-eat soup off the counter. I find bowls and reheat the food, bringing it out to the living room along with the rest of the food still in the bag.

Dean unfortunately put his shirt back on and he's sitting on the couch, looking relaxed and happy. It's a good look on him. I'm not sure I could ever get enough of it.

He smiles when his eyes meet mine, and he takes the bowls from me, setting them on the small coffee table.

We eat our soup, he feeds me egg rolls, and we finish watching *Love Actually*. Well, we sort of watch it. Our conversation starts with asking some basic "getting to know you better" questions, like what's your favorite color (mine is purple, his is black), and then dissolves into ridiculousness.

"What would you rather eat, an earthworm or a beetle?" I ask him.

"What kind of effed up question is that?"

"This is serious. I'll know whether you prefer crunchy food to soft and squishy food."

He eats a spoonful of soup and thinks for a few seconds before saying, "Then I have to go with the beetle. Soft and squishy sounds disturbing. There's a lot to be said for texture. What about you?"

"Totally the beetle, I've seen pictures of earthworms that are like five feet long. What if you had to eat that? I think the biggest beetle is like seven inches. Much more doable."

"So you're saying bigger isn't always better?"

"Not when it comes to the consumption of gross animal species."

After the food is gone, we both clean up the mess.

"Okay," I say as Dean's washing the bowls and I'm putting the bags in the trash. "Would you rather drink a cup of pee, or lick a homeless guy's ass?"

"You're disturbed."

"What, you can't handle the question?" I face him with my hand on my hip.

"I can handle the question." He finishes stacking the dishes in the dishwasher and dries his hands on a towel, leaning back against the counter and watching me.

"How big is this cup of pee, and can I get the homeless guy to shower and disinfect first?" he asks.

I laugh. "Now you're thinking."

He shakes his head. "If I'm thinking like you, something's seriously wrong with me."

25

Little minds are tamed and subdued by misfortune; but great minds rise above them.

–Washington Irving

Freya

A persistent banging rouses me from sleep. What the hell is that noise?

I slept like the dead. I haven't moved from the position I fell asleep in, cradled against Dean's chest, in his bed.

I lean back slightly and watch him sleep like the giant creeper I am. This is where I should probably wax on and on about how sweet and handsome he looks while he's sleeping, but really he looks like a slack-jawed yokel.

Somehow, it's still cute.

I slide out from under his arm without waking him up and walk over to his laptop where you can see the video from the front door.

The figure banging on the door is familiar to me. Lucy. What the heck is she doing here? Right when I finish the thought, she looks up at the camera and waves.

I find my clothes strewn about the room and quickly shrug them on before shutting Dean in the bedroom to sleep, and heading to the front door.

I unlock and open the door and Lucy lets out a breath when she sees me.

"You're here," she says.

"Yeah, come in, come in." I usher her inside and shut and lock the door behind her. "What's going on?"

"I've been trying to call you," she says.

"Oh." I haven't even thought about my cell phone in the last week. "My phone is on the charger I think. I haven't turned it on since we got back last night."

"I have to tell you something. Maybe you should sit down."

"Um, okay." We sit in the living room on the couch.

Lucy takes a breath and holds it, not saying anything, just watching me with an odd expression on her face.

"Lucy, you look like you have to take a giant dump. You're acting even weirder than normal. What's wrong?"

"It's Cameron."

"What about Cameron?"

"He's dead."

"What?"

"He's dead," she says, a little bit louder and slower.

"Shut the fuck up."

She blinks at me.

"I-I don't mean that literally. It's just, I can't believe this. How? Why? When?"

"He was shot. I don't know why. It happened last night. The time of death was between eight and ten in the evening. A bit earlier than the last murders."

I can't do anything but stare at her. I'm not exactly sure how I should take this news. Cameron was a bastard, and I may have wished—metaphorically and in passing—that he would disappear forever, but...dead? For reals?

"How did you...?"

"I purchased a police scanner after the shooting incident."

"Of course you did."

"The police are on their way here now. They've obtained a warrant for Dean's arrest."

And with that bombshell I'm struck speechless.

A sound at the bedroom door distracts me from Lucy for a moment. It's Dean, leaning against the doorframe in dark, low-slung jeans and a gray T-shirt, arms crossed over his chest, looking entirely too attractive.

"How long have you been standing there?" I ask.

"Long enough." He looks at Lucy. "How much time do you think I have?"

There's a loud knock at the door and a muffled voice says, "Open up, it's the police."

"Not much," Lucy says.

Dean straightens and looks at me. I stand but I can't move.

"This is all my fault," I say.

"No." He moves over to me and hugs me against his chest. "It's not your fault. Stay with Lucy, or stay here. Don't do anything crazy, you understand?" He pulls away far enough to look in my eyes.

"I'll stay with Lucy, but I'm not promising anything else," I say, and my voice only warbles a little bit.

The banging on the door gets louder, harder.

Dean's eyes focus on me with even more intensity. "I mean it, Freya. Don't put yourself in any danger. Don't make me worry about you more than I already will." He kisses me hard on the mouth, the action all too brief, before moving towards the door. He stops for a moment and puts a hand on Lucy's shoulder. "Take care of her," he says, his voice stern.

Lucy nods, and he opens the door.

I can't watch. I think I might be crying because everything seems blurry and surreal as the cops cuff Dean and take him away, reading the Miranda rights like they do in the movies, which makes me feel like maybe this isn't really happening. But all too soon, he's gone.

Then a detective is standing in front of me and telling me I need to go down to the station for questioning, and I absolutely have to or else I could be charged with obstruction of justice. Lucy agrees to drive me, and the drive happens in a blink of motion that I remember nothing of.

And then it's just me and Lucy and the hum of the air

conditioning in a small room that looks exactly like the interrogation room I rescued Dean from.

I'm not sure how much time passes. I feel shell shocked and exhausted.

The next thing I know, Lucy is handing me a glass of water, and then Detective Hanson is sitting in front of me. She's not as casual as the last time I saw her. Instead of jeans, she's wearing dark slacks and a blazer.

"Freya, right?" she asks.

I nod.

"I just have a few questions for you. What's your relationship with Dean Collins?" she asks, getting right down to business.

"He's my boyfriend."

"And what was your relationship with Cameron Myers?"

I glance at Lucy. She gives me an encouraging nod.

"He's my ex-boyfriend."

"Have they ever met?"

I hesitate. "I-I think so."

"Would you say their relationship was amicable?"

I know exactly where she's going with this. "Look, Dean didn't kill anyone. He was with me all last night. So before you go making assumptions, he has an alibi."

"Would you say that you're a credible witness?"

"Well, yes, of course."

She just stares at me, her expression blank.

"I'm not lying!" I say loudly.

"I didn't say that you were. But didn't you also impersonate a lawyer for the sole purpose of getting Dean out of questioning with this very same department?"

"Um, I..."

"It's a yes or no question, Miss Morgan."

Now I'm Miss Morgan? I never told her my last name. "Yes," I say, pushing away the nervous thought that this woman has been investigating me. "That doesn't change the fact that we were together last night. All night long."

We're screwed. There's no other suspects. Once again, Dean is a connection to the victim and I'm the least reliable witness in the history of all witnesses everywhere. And it's my own fault I suck.

"Did Dean leave the apartment last night at any time, for any reason?"

Shit. He left to get food. Should I leave that out? Should I pretend I forgot?

No. I can't lie. They must have the videos he has running constantly monitoring his front door. If they got a warrant for his arrest, they got a warrant to search his apartment. They know he left. They know how long he was gone. Lying will just make us appear guilty.

"He left to get dinner," I say reluctantly. "But he wasn't gone long," I add quickly.

"He went to The Golden Flower. Do you know how long it takes to get there from his apartment?"

"Um. A few minutes?"

"Right. And you ordered ahead."

"And?"

"And we've reviewed the tapes from the restaurant.

There's a twenty-minute time frame that we can't account for."

I hesitate, risking another glance at Lucy. Her mouth is drawn in a straight line, expression blank.

"Why are you telling me this?"

She shrugs. "Just wondering if maybe you can account for that time. We know you were in the apartment the entire time he was gone, the tapes prove that, and his cell phone records show he didn't call you while he was gone so..."

"So what?"

"So, it doesn't take much time to shoot someone in the head."

"He didn't do it! I know he didn't!"

She seems almost sympathetic. "It doesn't matter what you know. What matters is what you can prove."

"You're right. Can I go now?" I stand up and Lucy stands with me.

"Where are you going?"

"I may not be able to prove to you that Dean is innocent. But maybe I can prove that someone else is guilty."

Lucy speaks up for the first time. "Aren't you a member of the vice department, Detective Hanson?" she asks.

"Yes."

"Why is vice involved in homicide?"

Detective Hanson smiles at her. "There are some offenses that overlap."

She doesn't elaborate, and after a second Lucy nods and turns towards the door. I follow her.

"Miss Morgan," Detective Hanson says, when I've

opened the door and nearly stepped across the threshold. "You realize that we didn't have a motive until this last incident."

"What do you mean?"

"With the prior murders, all we were missing was motive. There was no logical reason for Dean to want them dead. But with this murder, there is a motive. You."

"Me?"

"You and your history with the victim. He had ample reason to want to hurt him, after the way he treated you."

A chill runs down my body.

"How do you know anything about that?" I ask.

"I read your statement from the shooting. I doubt that was an isolated incident."

"That doesn't mean Dean killed him."

"Don't you think it's possible he was protecting you?"

I consider it, for a brief, flickering moment.

"Would Dean hurt someone to protect me? Yes, undoubtedly. Would he go after someone unprovoked and kill them in cold blood? Absolutely not," I answer, making sure I'm looking the detective in the eye before I turn and walk out, Lucy on my heels.

We've barely made it three steps when the detective calls after us. "Ladies," she says. "I shouldn't have told you Cameron was shot in the head. That's classified information at this point. We haven't told the press, and no one knows. Please keep it under your hat."

We nod.

"And Miss Morgan?"

I turn around and meet her eyes.

"There's still hope. We haven't found the gun, yet."

I nod and we leave.

When we get back to Lucy's I throw myself on her couch, and almost immediately a giant fart noise rips through the air.

I frown. That wasn't me.

Lucy groans.

"I am so sorry." She shoves her hand under the cushion directly underneath me and pulls out a whoopee cushion. "Sam stopped by earlier, I should have known he would leave something behind."

I can't help it. I start laughing. I laugh so hard, I cry. And then I go from crying from laughter to crying for reals because goddammit, Dean's in jail and there's nothing I can do about it.

I totally lose my shit, and I lose it good. There's tears, slobber, snot, all kinds of bodily fluids. I'm lucky I don't piss my pants.

Lucy does way better than she did the first time she saw me have a meltdown. Instead of trying to solve my problem right away with logical thinking, she lets me get it out, all over her couch, while she pats my back. It's only slightly awkward as opposed to completely awkward. She's getting better.

When I'm finished I just lie there and stare up at her slowly rotating ceiling fan. I can't believe this is happening. This is horrible, and it's all my fault. I never should have got mixed up with him in the first place. If I hadn't hired him all those months ago, he wouldn't be rotting away in some cell somewhere. What if he's convicted and sent to prison? What about his family? What if I never see him again? Dammit. I should have jumped his bones when I had the chance.

"Do they allow conjugal visits in jail?" I ask Lucy.

She frowns. "You're thinking about that now?"

"It's either that or spiral into self-loathing and despair."

"We need to make a list of potential suspects."

"We've tried that. We have no links between the first two victims, except Dean. Daisy was a potential suspect, but she has no reason to kill Matt or Cameron, that we know of. Cameron has a connection to Matt via Liz, but why? And now he's dead. Unless we can prove he killed Jesse and Matt and then offed himself?" I sigh. "It's impossible. They still don't have the gun, and I doubt his ghost moved it from the scene of the crime."

She shakes her head. "Let's focus on the charge against Dean. Who wanted to kill Cameron?"

I snort. "That's gonna be a long-ass list. Might as well put me at the top."

Lucy sighs and stands up, leaving me on the couch while she grabs her laptop. She sits in the chair opposite me and starts typing away.

I lie there, staring into space, not really seeing anything. I can't think enough to help. I'm drained. Exhausted. Pathetic. My brain is mush.

An unknown length of time later, Lucy lets out a frustrated groan.

"What is it?" I ask.

"I've been reviewing the security tapes around campus from the nights of the three murders. Cameron was at the library the night of both murders. He left at closing. When I reviewed the closing tapes for the nights in between the murders, he was never there. It's an odd coincidence. And irritating because he's deceased and therefore not available for questioning."

She continues clicking away, pausing to read and review whatever she's looking at.

More time passes, and I think I doze off because the next thing I know, Lucy is shaking me awake. "Jensen's home and he brought pizza," she says.

"I'm not hungry." I sit up and rub the sleep from my eyes.

"Wow. Has hell frozen over?" Jensen asks from the doorway to the kitchen. It's nearly dark outside. I must have been out for a while.

I smile weakly. "Possibly."

He flicks on the light in the living room and brings out a plate for me anyway. "I'll just set it here and you can eat if the mood strikes you."

He disappears into the kitchen with Lucy and I can hear her speaking softly, explaining what's happened and what her research revealed this afternoon.

I feel useless. Lucy's here, helping me, and I'm like a slug of inadequacy and gloom.

They both come into the living room with plates of pizza and Jensen clicks on the TV, letting a sitcom run in the background while we eat. Well, while they eat and I try to eat.

"Wow. You definitely have it bad," Jensen says when they've finished their meals and I've only managed to choke down a couple of bites. "I never thought I would see the day."

"Laugh it up, chuckles. I'm glad you can derive amusement from my misery," I say weakly. I get what he's doing, trying to banter with me, make me feel better. I don't think anything can make me feel better.

He stands and takes Lucy's plate and then mine, patting me on the head and saying, "We'll figure this out Freya, no worries." Then he disappears into the kitchen.

The water turns on and the clank of plates being washed echoes into the living room.

"You've got a good man there," I tell Lucy.

She nods. "I know."

"Maybe someone will be murdered while Dean's in jail, then he'll have an airtight alibi and be exonerated," Jensen calls out.

"Like in that movie, *Scream*," I say to Lucy. She looks at me blankly. "You know, Ghostface?" She just shakes her head at me.

"Hello, Sydney," I say in my creepiest voice, which comes out more like a froggy voice.

She just lifts one eyebrow.

I sigh. You'd think I'd be used to explaining pop culture references to her by now. "So, this guy, like, calls these girls, asking what their favorite scary movie is and then he kills them while wearing a ghost mask and black cape thing." I frown. "I've always liked that movie but when I explain it, it sounds really lame. Anyway, Sydney is the main character and Ghostface busts into her house and tries to kill her. She calls the cops and her boyfriend shows up right before the police, so they suspect him. While he's in jail, the Ghostface makes a threatening phone call to Sydney. They knew it couldn't be the boyfriend, so they let him go." Something else occurs to me. "Except he does end up being the murderer—well, one of the murderers—because there's two guys working together."

At my last words our eyes meet and I can see the same thing flash in Lucy's mind that's flashing through mine.

"What if there's more than one murderer?" I say aloud.

She shakes her head. "Multiple killers in the same area killing coeds is statistically unlikely but...What if Cameron did kill the first two victims—or one of them, at least—and someone found out and killed him? Or killed him for some other reason?" Lucy asks. She plucks her laptop off the table and immediately begins typing.

"There are plenty of reasons to go around," I answer. "Considering his status as the Duke of Douche." I know you shouldn't speak ill of the dead and all that, but I've never understood that philosophy. An asshole who dies is still a dead asshole.

Lucy's nodding at me, typing into her computer, and stopping to read occasionally. I stand up, suddenly sick of moping on the couch and begin pacing in front of her. I run a frustrated hand through my hair. "But we're still getting nowhere. We don't know who had motive to kill

Cameron—it could be any number of skanks." I stop pacing. "Holy shit. What about Liz?"

"Liz?" Lucy looks up at me from the computer screen.

"Yes. I've seen her a couple times over the last few weeks. I bet she could help us compile a list of suspects. She broke up with Cameron recently and she's Matt's sister."

"Maybe she is a suspect."

I shrug. "I dunno. She's more of a lover than a fighter. I can't picture her shooting anyone. I can picture her sleeping with a whole lot of people, though." Cringe. "I don't want to think about that."

"We'll put her on the list because we can't discount any possibilities."

"I'll call her and meet her and see if I can wrangle some more names out of her."

Lucy nods. "Okay. Be careful and keep me apprised of your whereabouts at all times. Someone could still be after you, and I don't trust anyone. I'll research Liz and see if I can find any evidence of where she was the night of Cameron's murder."

I plop back down on the couch. I still feel like poop, but I like having a plan. Something to focus on. Other than Dean sitting in a cell.

26

In the time of darkest defeat, victory may be nearest.

–William McKinley

Freya

I text Liz the slut (I can't not think of her that way) and we agree to meet for coffee at a little café near campus.

"Thanks for inviting me. I really hope we can be friends again," she says after we've ordered our drinks and we're sitting at a little table in the corner.

"Of course," I say.

I really don't have any problem with her anymore. I mean, if you want to be a slut and sleep with guys who are taken, who am I to judge? Actually, I should be thanking her. If she hadn't slept with Cameron maybe I would have stayed with him, stuck in a terrible, never-ending relationship of doom.

"I heard about your brother. I'm really sorry," I tell her.

"Thanks," she says, staring down into her coffee and tucking a strand of dark hair behind her ear. "We were pretty close. Twins."

"Really?"

"Yeah. It's been weird since he's been gone. I almost don't believe it, you know? For the longest time, it's been just the two of us, and now..." she trails off.

"What about your parents?"

"No parents. They died and we went into foster care when we were kids."

And now I feel like the biggest bitch on the planet. Liz the slut is actually little orphan Lizzie?

I can't help but ask. "You didn't have any other relatives that could have taken you guys in?"

"Our parents were only children, and our grandparents are all dead. There was a distant cousin, somewhere, but I don't think they wanted us."

I don't know what to say at that. She basically just informed me that her only living relative just died. I might be a slut, too, if I had that type of upbringing.

"Crazy what happened to Cameron, huh?" she says, breaking the somewhat uncomfortable silence that sprouted up after her last statement.

It's weird to hear his name. I'm so used to Dean saying it wrong.

Dean.

I swallow. Need to focus on the task at hand.

"It is." I laugh a little, feeling a bit awkward, and shake my head. "Crazier than a tarantula on skis." I'm staring down into my coffee, but raise my eyes to hers before saying, "I'm glad you mentioned him though—"

"I'm sorry," she interrupts quickly. "I'm sorry about that whole thing. I know I apologized before, but...I was such an idiot. I never should have dated him, especially while you were also dating him and I knew that." She sighs and shakes her head. "I was going through this phase up till... well, now, where I didn't feel good about myself unless I could make a guy like me, and it didn't matter who he was or who I hurt. The bigger the challenge the better. I've changed though, honestly."

I smile at her since she seems so nervous. "It's water under the bridge. Apology accepted."

"Thank you." She smiles and her shoulders relax with the movement, like a burden has been lifted. She reaches to cover my hand with hers and instead knocks my coffee right off the side of the table. "Omigosh!" She stands, grabbing towels from the little dispenser, knocking that to the ground too, attempting to sop up the mess that's dripping onto the floor. "I'm so nervous, I can't believe I just did that, here, you—you just stay here, I'll get another coffee."

"It's okay," I reassure her, grabbing the napkin dispenser from the ground and helping her clean up the mess.

"I'll just—I'll be right back." She laughs, quick and sharp, her face flushing in embarrassment.

She walks over to the counter and orders another cup from the barista while I finish sopping up what's left of the liquid on the table with a cheap napkin that dissolves as I'm wiping.

She seems entirely too nervous for a simple, friendly coffee date. Oh wait. Date? I really hope she doesn't think that this is *that* kind of date. Maybe when she said she's changed, she meant she's batting for the other team? Should I tell her I don't think of her that way?

When she returns, she sets the coffee in front of me.

"Thank you, you didn't have to do that," I say.

She waves me off and there's a moment of silence while we sip our drinks.

I turn the subject back to why I asked her here in the first place. "About Cameron," I say. "You actually did me a favor." I laugh and fiddle with what's left of a wet napkin on the table. "He was such a jerk, right?"

"Totally!" She laughs and shakes her head. "I have no idea what I saw in him." Something dark passes through her eyes, and I wonder if she had a similar experience to mine, but I can't think of that right now and this is neither the time nor the place. Now, I need to see if she knows who would want him dead. I can do this. I'll ease her into it.

"So who do you think killed him?"

Maybe *plunge* would be better.

"Um." She laughs again. "I have no idea. Didn't they pick up that guy that runs the boxing matches every weekend? I guess he was implicated in those other murders." She shrugs. "Who cares, at this point, right?"

I care! But I don't want to tell her that. I don't know why. She seems perfectly sincere, but I feel like what I have with Dean is my little secret and Liz the slut is the last person I want to know because she'll do something to try and ruin it. Okay. Maybe that water isn't quite running under the bridge as smoothly as I suggested.

She changes the subject to school—I didn't realize she was in nursing school—and her internship at the hospital. She goes on and on for about five minutes about how she has to change a diaper for some old guy who keeps getting an erection, when I have to cut her off. By now, the caffeine from all the coffee should be hitting my bloodstream, but I'm getting more tired than anything. That's weird.

"So, since you work at the hospital, did you see Cameron the night he died?"

"No, I didn't work that night."

"But did you hear about Cameron's autopsy or anything?"

"Please," she scoffs. "Pretty sure Cameron was DOA. They only autopsy if foul play is suspected or they can't determine the cause of death. It's pretty obvious when someone is shot in the head."

"Right," I smile and stare down into my coffee. It's making pretty swirls. Did she get me a cappuccino? The kind where they make the foam into pretty stuff?

Wait. Back the truck up.

"How did you know he was shot in the head?" I ask. My tongue feels thick in my mouth. Am I slurring?

"What?" she asks.

"The detective told us that that information wasn't

released to the press. She told us, but she shouldn't have told us." Now my coffee isn't just swirling, there's literally colors flying off the top, like steam. Rainbow steam.

"This has been really great," Liz says suddenly. "I have to go. Why don't I walk you to your car?"

"Um." I rub my eyes. They feel tired. And they just feel. Isn't that weird? Feeling your eyeballs. I should definitely get home. "Right. Thanks." I stand and feel immediately dizzy.

"Here, let me help you." Liz rushes over to my side.

"That's strange," I say when I blink and we're outside standing next to the open backseat door of a car. It's not my car.

"Where's my car?"

Liz smiles at me, but it doesn't reach her eyes. "Don't worry about it. Just get in."

Something is wrong, but my mind is feeling too fuzzy to pick out what it is. This is just like the other time when Cameron drugged me! But wait...

"You," I say to Liz as she gently puts me in the backseat of her car. My arms feel like noodles and my legs are rubber. I can't get out. I can't fight back. "You're the douche," I manage just before everything goes black.

When I regain consciousness, my neck hurts, my arms are numb and I have a searing headache.

"Holy fucking shark week!"

"You've always had a way with words."

I blink my eyes open against bright lights. I'm tied in a chair, in some kind of basement or storage room from the looks of it, and Liz is standing in front of me. There's a table between us and a bag resting on that. She's pulling out a syringe and filling it with some liquid from a jar, squeezing the plunger top until liquid squirts out the end of the needle. Her hands are encased in surgical gloves.

I glance around the dark room. The walls and floor are concrete. I can't see much beyond the circle of light above me.

"Don't worry," she says, stepping around the table towards me, needle in hand. "It's not what you think." She stops in front of me.

"You aren't going to kill me?" I can't look at her face. I can only look at the sharp pointy thing, glistening in the light.

"No."

I sag in the chair. "Oh, thank God. For a second I thought this was going to turn into a whole *Saw* thing and the key just went down the drain, and we'd have to kill each other or something."

She sits on the small table and faces me, saying nothing, making me nervous.

"If you're not going to kill me, why all the theatrics?" I ask.

"It's the only way to make sure your boyfriend is acquitted. If they think the killer is still on the loose and got away, and you can give them misleading details…" she trails off and shrugs. "This is just a sedative." She lifts the needle and I lean back involuntarily.

"It's the same sedative I used on Cameron, before I killed him. If they do an autopsy after this, they'll find the connection."

And with that bombshell, I look her in the eyes. "Did you kill Jesse and Matt, too?"

"No. I don't know who killed Jesse, but I know who killed Matt."

"Cameron?"

"The one and only."

I shake my head, but it hurts when I move it so I stop on a wince. "Why?" I ask.

"You got out before he got real bad." She lets out a small laugh that's so devoid of humor it could be a sob. "You have no idea what he was really like. And what he did to you was small potatoes. Following you. Going to your house, shooting up your car. That was nothing."

I don't say anything. I'm thinking over her words. I remember being followed, the night I called Dean and agreed to help him. That was Cameron? And now I know who shot at me and Dean.

She stares down at the floor for what feels like forever, but is probably just a minute before she swallows and starts talking, gaze still downward.

"After you saw us in his dorm room, he stopped talking to me, for a while. Then, all of a sudden—I assume it was after you broke up with him—he came back to me all apologies and sweetness. We were together for a little bit, and then he started asking me to do things. You know, in bed. It started out pretty innocent. Well, I thought it was innocent. Just some role-playing. I would pretend to resist and...he really got off on it."

I can't help but cringe.

She looks up and meets my eyes. "I thought the allure would fade after a bit, but it just got worse. And worse, and worse. It didn't help when he got hooked on Devil's Gate and everything escalated. He became paranoid. Overbearing. Insane."

Devil's Gate. That's the drug the detective talked about.

Her free hand starts fiddling with a tear in her jeans. "He got progressively more violent. I didn't know what to do. It turned into one of those stupid relationships, and I was the stupid girl who couldn't get out. At first he told me he would hurt me if I left, and when I was gonna leave anyway, he told me he would hurt others. My brother. My friends."

I don't say anything else, waiting for her to continue.

"One night, it got really bad. I thought I was going to die. It was the night he killed Matt. He got set off because I was going to leave. Matt had convinced me that it wasn't worth it, that I could stay with him and he would protect me. This was just after I saw you at the restaurant. I went to pack up my stuff, but Cameron came over. I told him it was over, he threatened me, and I told him I would go to the cops if he tried anything. He locked me in the bathroom for three days."

"Three days? Didn't anyone notice you were gone?"

She shrugs. "It was a Friday. He didn't let me out until Monday morning so I could go to class. But I missed that day. I was starving and exhausted and when I found out about Matt…" She shakes her head and wipes the tears falling down her cheeks with the back of her hand. "He knew, you see. Cameron knew if he killed Matt, he wouldn't only have control over me, he knew it would implicate your little boyfriend. I didn't know that part until recently, though. But I knew, then, that I couldn't just leave. I would have to plan and wait, and if I couldn't get the cops to arrest him or charge him or whatever, then I would have to kill him myself. I couldn't let him keep on going. Then he started doing this." She lifts up her shirt to reveal a series of cuts across her abdomen, along her side where the skin is especially sensitive. Some of the wounds are old and healed, but there are a couple that are still red and scabbed.

"He gave me this one," she trails her finger across a particularly thick patch of scarred skin, "before he locked me in the bathroom."

"I get why you did it." I swallow and look away when she lowers her shirt. "I can't say I blame you. I just can't believe it."

"I really tried to get the attention of the detectives on the case. Cameron was getting more and more out of control with the drugs and his obsession with you. It was almost a good thing—for me—because he stopped caring so much about what I was doing and I could get away with more. I've been sending anonymous letters, making phone calls with voice modulators…and nothing. They had no evidence. It was my word against his, and I was too scared to come forward publicly. He would have killed me, for sure."

"It was you that drugged me at the bar that night."

She nods.

"Why?"

"I was trying to set him up. I know how he is and he totally still had a thing for you, since you rejected him. You wouldn't have been hurt. I was going to call the cops and they would have shown up before anything happened. I just wanted him to be caught, but then things kept getting in the way. Your boyfriend, the stupidity of the damn cops in this town. He was after you, you know. He tried to follow you home one night, and he got pissed when he found out you had a boyfriend and tried to kill both of you.

"Finally, I saw my chance, and I took it. He didn't suffer. I drugged him and then shot him in the head with his own gun to make it look like the other murders. But I didn't realize that my actions would also implicate your..." She waves her hand in my direction.

"Boyfriend," I say flatly.

"Right. I didn't know the suspect was the same guy you were shacking up with until it was too late. So then I had to fix it."

"And this is how you fix it?" I can't move my arms, so I try to gesture with my head.

She shrugs. "I had to make it believable. Now, I'll knock you out." She points the needle at me. "When they find you, tell them it was some raving madman who was going to kill you but then you blacked out and he was gone."

"That's not gonna work!"

"Sure it will. They can't blame you. You couldn't have

tied yourself up, and they can't blame your man because he definitely has a solid alibi this time. And I'll be long gone."

She steps towards me with the needle.

"Are you sure all of this drugging won't damage me in some way?"

"Yes."

"Is it really necessary?"

"Yes. It's the same thing I used to drug Cameron and they'll be able to verify that."

"Where are you going to go?"

"Like I'm going to tell you that. Don't worry about me, I'll go somewhere no one will be able to find me. No one cares enough to look, anyway. I've been planning this for a while."

I take a deep breath. This is crazy, but fuck it. What do I have to lose? "Do it quick. I don't think you have much time."

"Why do you say that?"

"Lucy can GPS my cell."

Her eyes widen. "Seriously?"

"Yes. She didn't trust you. She promised Dean she would keep an eye on me, and she doesn't really trust me either."

She smiles. "Smart girl."

That's when we hear it, a shuffling sound coming from somewhere behind me. I'm not sure what's behind me, but when I hear a brisk knock, I have to assume that's where the door is.

Liz's eyes widen.

"They're here," I say.

"Yep."

She doesn't turn around, even when a muffled voice calls out behind me, "Open up. Police."

"What are you going to do?" I ask her.

She shrugs, her face resigned. "Change of plans."

She moves quickly—there's a pinch on my shoulder, and I'm out for the count. Again.

27

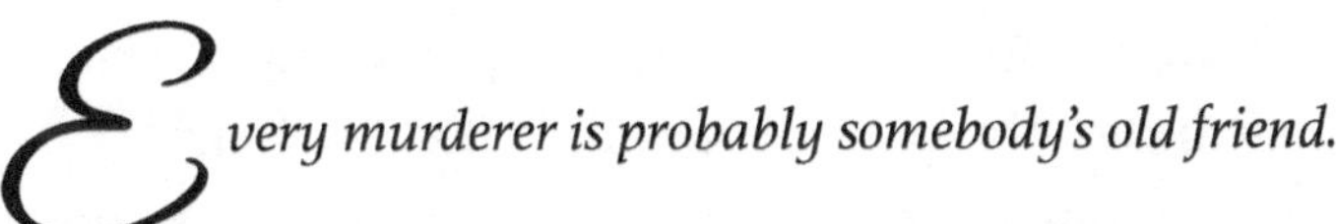

Every murderer is probably somebody's old friend.

–Agatha Christie

Dean

Have I mentioned how much I hate hospitals? It's almost worse than jail. In jail, I got three hots and a cot. For free.

It's the middle of the night. Freya is sleeping. She's been unconscious since they found her. My heart clenches and my stomach threatens to expel its contents every time I think about what could have happened.

I was released after they found her, and I came directly to the hospital. I've called her mother and she's driving in tonight, but probably won't be here until tomorrow.

Lucy and Jensen were at the hospital when I arrived, but I sent them home. Now I'm sitting beside Freya's bed with my head on her mattress, holding her limp hand.

I probably shouldn't be here, probably not allowed since the terms of visiting hours don't apply to a boyfriend, but the nurses here know me from the amount of times I've been here with my mom and they haven't given me any flak.

I'm falling asleep, the steady beep-beep-beeping of Freya's heart monitor lulling me into a light stupor but then something moves against my hand.

I jerk away with a groan and sit up, moving my hand from hers and rubbing my eyes against the dim light.

I hear a strange croak and it sounds like Freya's trying to say my name.

"Freya?"

"Mmhmm," she manages. I can see her eyes are open and a wave of relief crashes over me.

"Oh, thank God." I grab her hand again and squeeze.

She tries to speak, but all that comes out is more croaking.

"What do you need? Water? Here." I flick on the light next to the bed and fumble with some buttons, working them until I get the correct one that pushes her into a sitting position. Then I grab a cup of water from the side table and hold it up for her, positioning the straw into her mouth.

She takes a few small swallows and sits back.

"Better?" I ask, placing the cup back on the bedside

table and taking her hand, rubbing her knuckles with my thumb. I am never letting her go again.

"Yes," she says, and the word is fairly legible. "What happened?" she asks.

"You don't remember anything?"

"I…" she pauses, her eyes searching mine as she tries to remember. She looks tired. Her eyes are a little swollen, but to me, she looks perfect. Her eyes widen as she remembers. "They took you to jail! But you're here now."

"Yes," I say carefully and then I wait to see if more will come back. I don't know exactly what she went through—no one does yet.

"Lucy and I talked to the detectives after they took you away. We went to her place, and we decided to try to get a list of suspects from Liz."

I can almost see the memories as they hit her. Her eyes widen and her breathing accelerates, so does her heart monitor. I rub her hand gently, willing her to calm down so the nurse doesn't come in.

"Where is she?" she asks. "The last thing I remember is the cops at the door and the drugs going into my arm."

I tell her as much as I know. "She's in ICU. She injected herself with a syringe full of air."

"What? Why?"

"We were hoping you could tell us. The detectives have been checking in every hour, waiting for you to wake up."

She haltingly relates her experiences over the last twenty-four hours, getting coffee, everything Liz revealed to her about the murders and that goddamn asswipe

Cameron. She only stops once halfway through for another drink to soothe her throat.

"What happened when the cops found us?" she asks when she's done.

"Well. Liz turned the needle on herself, but not before filling it with air and putting it in her veins."

"Why would she do that?"

I shrug, tightening my hand on hers. "Probably because she got caught and she prefers death to prison. If you inject an air bubble into the right artery, it can stop your heart. But the odds are slim of something like that actually working, unless the person has a preexisting heart condition."

"They can't put her in prison."

"She admitted to premeditated murder, and she kidnapped and drugged you."

"Yeah, but it was to save you. And she had a good reason to kill Cameron. He was psychotic."

"I'm not disagreeing with you, but you know how the law is."

"Yeah."

She looks so tired.

"Sleep," I say, letting go of her hand to readjust the bed before clicking the light back off. I stand up to move into the chair.

"Wait, where are you going?" she asks, her voice panicked.

"Nowhere, just going to sit in the chair over here."

"Oh. Okay."

I sit down and listen to her breathing. After a few

minutes, it seems like she's falling asleep, but then she jerks awake with a moan.

"Are you okay?" I ask, leaning forward in the chair.

She's silent for a moment and then she asks, "Will you...will you lie with me?"

I step closer to the bed. "I'm not sure I'll fit," I say with a smile.

She rolls over onto my side to make space behind in the narrow hospital bed. I walk around to avoid lying on the side with the IV and after a bit of maneuvering, I manage to lie down behind her, arm draped over her waist, body cupped around hers.

"Is this okay?" I whisper into her ear.

"Perfect. I'm sorry. I dreamt that Cameron was standing at the foot of my bed staring at me while I slept."

"No need to apologize. And that was me staring at you while you slept."

She puts her hand over mine where it's settled at her waist.

"Except it's so much less creepy when it's you."

I smile against her hair, breathing in her scent which smells like her shampoo.

Wrapped up as we are, it doesn't take long for both of us to relax into each other and drift into sleep.

I fall asleep with a smile on my face and the one thought that's putting it there.

She's going to be okay.

The next morning, Detective Hanson comes to see Freya at the hospital to ask follow-up questions. She's kind of intense, but I don't mind that so much now that she's not trying to put me in jail.

Freya wants me to stay in the room with her while she tells her side of the story. I sit on the edge of her bed, holding her hand while she repeats everything she told me last night. Then the detective fills us in on the details we missed.

"So Daisy killed Jesse, Cameron killed Matt, and Liz killed Cameron," I say, after she's explained everything that she can to us.

"From what we've gathered, yes, that's correct," Detective Hanson says.

I can't believe it.

"Three killers," Freya says.

"Two of whom were using Devil's Gate, which is a highly addictive, paranoia-inducing narcotic." The detective shakes her head. "It makes people who might otherwise react rationally, become violent and reckless."

"Daisy didn't seem terribly reckless. Her plan was pretty well thought out," Freya says.

"According to her revised statement, she and her friends were doing drugs and partying. She went into the bathroom, got sick, and then when she got the text from Dean," she motions towards me, "she walked right out the front door. Her friends didn't even notice because they were all too intoxicated. Her brother's gun was in her trunk because he had been using her car and he had been attempting to sell the firearm. She found Jesse, shot him, and then went back to the party and passed out. She didn't even remember what she had done until she heard about the killing the next afternoon."

I grimace. "This drug sounds terrible."

"It's not good. We've been trying to get a handle on it for a few months now."

There's a pause in our conversation when a nurse comes in to take Freya's blood pressure and temperature.

"How's Liz?" Freya asks as the nurse leaves.

Detective Hanson takes a breath and looks at both of us before saying, "She's gone."

"Gone?" I ask.

"She left the hospital in the middle of the night. We had a guard watching over her, but somehow she snuck past him."

Freya shakes her head. "I can't say I'm surprised. She had more tricks up her sleeve than I ever realized."

"Doesn't she need more medical treatment?" I ask.

Detective Hanson gives a helpless shrug. "You'd think so. She was pregnant. Did she tell you?"

Freya gasps and her hand tightens in mine. "No." She shakes her head. "The baby has got to be Cameron's. Probably. I mean, she made it sound like she had traded her slutty ways for a life of domestic violence."

"She didn't, by any chance, tell you where she might have gone? Or do you have any ideas?"

"No..." Freya says, thinking. "Well, she told me that she would go somewhere she couldn't be found, and that she'd been planning it for a while, but she never said where."

The detective nods and looks down at the notepad in her hands. “We’ll track her down.”

“What will happen to her, when you find her?” I ask.

Her eyes meet mine. “She’ll be charged with murder and fleeing to avoid prosecution.”

“But the murder was self-defense,” Freya says.

“That’s not for me to decide. It’s up to a jury of her peers. If she gets a good lawyer, maybe they can prove justifiable homicide. Either way.” She shrugs. “It doesn’t look good that she ran.”

“It seems so unfair. It doesn’t seem right. It doesn’t seem like justice,” Freya says.

After the detective leaves, Freya sleeps and I watch her doze while I think over everything that’s happened.

I can’t believe the events of the past couple months. The bad was very bad, and the good was very good. I suppose you can’t have one without the other. I choose to focus on the good and be grateful that everyone I love is alive and well.

No regrets.

28

If you take no risks, you will suffer no defeats. But if you take no risks, you win no victories.

–Richard Nixon

Freya

"What are we doing here?" I ask when Dean pulls his car up outside the old warehouse. It looks different during the day. The last time I was here was at night, the first time I met Dean.

"I have a surprise for you." He flashes me a smile before sliding out of the driver's side door and walking around to open my door for me.

"You're going to make me wrestle Lucy in a pool full of

Jell-O?" I ask when I notice Jensen's car parked amongst the rest of the vehicles.

"That's a tempting idea, but no." He takes my hand and leads me away from the car, shutting the door behind me.

"Is this what you've been working on?"

After the whole murder thing blew over and we got through the rest of the semester and finals, Dean spent most of the summer working on some secret project. He's been really tight-lipped about it, only telling me that it's a surprise and he'll show me when it's ready.

It's been quite a summer. I've spent most of it with Dean, either at his place or mine. We took a quick trip to my mom's house one weekend, and we've spent a fair amount of time with his mom and sister. It's been idyllic, really. Except for one thing.

We still haven't had sex. I guess it's not that big of a problem. We've done everything else, but I love Dean. I'm ready to share everything with him. I haven't told him yet—that I love him or that I want to bang him—and to be fair, he hasn't said anything to me, either. Not since that one night when he said he would do anything for me and since then...radio silence. Well, not silence of course. I mean, we talk, but not about that. I'm trying not to read too much into it. I know he's giving me space, but the wait is killing me at this point. I've been dropping subtle hints, sleeping next to him in barely there tank tops and flimsy panties. His response? Nothing. Well, hardly anything. He's like a monk.

We reach the door and he swings it open to reveal that the space has been transformed into...

"A gym?" I look up at him while we're still standing in the doorway.

He smiles down at me. "Not just any gym."

Still holding the door, he gestures for me to enter.

The ring is still in the back of the large space, standing empty. The front of the giant room has been broken off into different sections. I notice Jose—the ref from the first night I met Dean—standing in one of the sections with a group of college girls and it looks like he's showing them how to fight.

He's still wearing too-tight boy shorts, but this time they're purple instead of hot pink.

In one of the other sections near a wall, I spot Lucy. She's wearing her lab coat and eye goggles, and she's surrounded by a group of young girls. There's a sink in her section and a small fridge.

"What is Lucy doing?"

He chuckles and shakes his head. "She's going over the physics of pepper spray, and how to make it yourself from items commonly found in one's kitchen."

There's other groups of people in different areas. Some spaces are empty, and there's a section that has free weights and varying exercise machines.

"What is this place?"

"It's a self-defense school for women."

"Really?"

"Yes." He smiles down at me and takes my hand in his, absently kissing the back of my hand before continuing. "It's also a gym. The ladies can work out, take classes. Due to high demand, I've even started a boxing class for women over sixty."

I laugh. "Shut up."

He shrugs. "I thought I could put my skills to better use."

"I can't believe this is what you've been working on." I gaze up at him.

"You like it?"

"Like it? I love it!"

He takes me around, showing me the different areas and what each of them can be used for.

Once he's nearly finished, and we're closer to the ring, I cut him off.

"Come on," I say, grabbing his hand and pulling him through the crowd, waving to Lucy along the way, and then dragging him into the little room where we first met.

It looks basically the same. There's still a solitary light bulb overhead that clicks on when I fumble for the switch on the wall, and the metal bench against the wall, next to a steel countertop. Except now it seems to be used for storage. There's a few first-aid kits on the counter, and some boxing gloves and safety pads stacked in the corner.

"What are we doing?" he asks.

"Nothing," I say, locking the door behind us before I grab his head and kiss him. It doesn't take more than a second for him to get the idea.

His tongue slides against mine as he picks me up and walks me to the counter, setting me on top of it before stepping in between my legs. Things get heated quickly, like they normally do, and like he normally does, Dean steps away from me, leaning his forehead against mine, and taking a deep breaths to calm himself.

"No," I say, pulling his body back towards me with my legs by wrapping them around his waist.

I can feel proof between my legs that he wants this as much as I do.

"You're driving me banana-hammock crazy," I say.

"Am I?"

I pull my head back from his to look at his face. He's smiling.

"You're enjoying this," I accuse.

He rubs his hands over my back and down to my waist. "You have no idea how much."

"I mean, you like driving me nutso."

"Yep. That too."

"I'm not waiting anymore."

His smile grows. "You think *you're* the one that's been waiting?"

"Uh, yeah!" I smack him on the shoulder. "Why else do you think I've been wearing super uncomfortable lingerie to bed every night, and strutting around half naked every day?"

"Because you were trying to drive *me* crazy," he says.

"Well, yeah. Sort of. It's just that...I love you," I say.

Silence.

My face heats. I can't believe I said that. I can't meet his eyes. Instead, I stare down at our legs. I'm not sure I can take seeing his reaction so I keep talking. "And I'm not sure how good I am at making the first move. I thought you would get it by my actions and then you'd say something or do something."

"No," he says, his voice sounds a little hoarse. He clears it and then says, "I didn't get it. I'm a normal guy not a mind reader. You just have to tell me."

"Well, now I'm telling you." I'm still staring downward.

He cups his palms around my face and gently lifts my gaze upward.

Once we're looking each other in the eyes, he says, "I love you, too."

I smile. "Awesome. Now let's get it on." I immediately begin fumbling with his belt.

"Whoa there, tiger." He moves my hands away. "We are not having our first time on a metal table in a dirty room with a hundred people right outside the door."

"Why the hell not?"

He shakes his head. "You are so unromantic."

"Bullshit. Now take your clothes off."

He laughs.

"Come on." He steps back and grabs my hands to help me jump off the counter. "Let's go home."

The entire ride home I'm a bundle of nerves and anticipation. What if I suck in bed, and not in the good way that you can suck while in bed?

I mean, Cameron is the only person I've ever been with, and we only did it twice. Dean has probably done it loads of times. Just look at him.

At that thought my eyes are drawn to his profile. He's got such a great face, a strong jaw, beautiful cheek bones. Maybe I stare a little too long.

"You okay?" Dean glances over at me and then back at the road, his face concerned. "We don't have to do this, you know."

"Oh yes we do. We have to do this, or I might explode."

"As long as you don't explode in my car—I just washed it." He smiles.

I try to return it, but it must not look very convincing, because his grin falters right before he turns his gaze back to the road in front of us.

A few minutes later, he parks in front of my apartments, shuts the engine off, and then turns towards me.

"Tell me what's bothering you," he says, taking my hand in his.

"I might be bad in bed," I blurt quickly.

He laughs.

"This isn't funny." I try to pull my hand away, but he catches it and holds on a little tighter.

"Why would you think you're bad in bed? From what I've experienced so far, you have nothing to worry about." He pulls my hand up to his mouth and kisses my wrist.

"I slept with Cameron twice. The first time hurt terribly, and the second time it was against my will. Whereas you…" I trail off. I have no idea what his experience is, and I haven't asked. I don't want to know about all the hot chicks he's been with.

"Whereas I've slept with a veritable harem of women."

My mouth drops open. "You have?"

"No," he laughs. "Don't be ridiculous. I've been with two people. There was Angelica, of course, and then a one-night stand after we broke up. I don't recommend one-night stands, by the way. It wasn't that great, and the day after was horrible and awkward."

I frown at him, disbelieving. "That's it?"

"That's it."

Odd. "Okay."

"Do you feel better now?"

"Not really, I thought you were more experienced than that. At least one of us needs to know what to do!"

Now he's really laughing. "Will anything make you happy?" he asks.

"Kiss me." I lean my head back against the headrest.

He doesn't hesitate, immediately leaning towards me over the center console and kissing my lips gently.

"Better?" He leans back.

"No."

He grins. "Come on." He gets out of the car and walks around to open my door.

We're heading up the stairs when I notice he's kinda hunched and squirmy. "Why are you walking funny?"

"I'm a little…excited."

I snort out a laugh and stop walking. "Really?"

"Yes, really, now hurry up before I carry you up these steps."

I stay put.

He laughs softly and shakes his head. "You're enjoying this way too much," he says as he reaches towards me and swings me up into his arms.

"Yep." I snuggle into him, wrapping my arms around his neck.

It gets cumbersome when we have to unlock my door because I won't let him put me down. Somehow, we make it inside. After I lock the door behind us, he runs us into the bedroom and chucks me on the bed, crawling immediately over me.

I have to laugh at his eagerness as his body covers mine and he starts kissing me. He's finally, finally, FINALLY going to put out.

His hands span my waist, fingers pressing gently under the hem of my shirt.

"You're so tiny," he says.

"I'm normal size. You're a giant."

He chuckles. "Let's hope you continue to think so once you've seen all of me," he winks and gives me a cheeky grin.

I laugh. "I've seen enough. I don't think I'll be too disappointed."

"Not *too* disappointed?"

"Right, just moderately disappointed."

He shakes his head solemnly. "That is so not funny."

I reach up and trace a finger down his jawline to his lips, covering them gently with a finger. "No more talky talky," I whisper.

He laughs, jarring my hand away and I scoot up to press my mouth against his.

He presses back, and we sink into the mattress together.

Our clothes disappear an item at a time. His shirt. My shirt. My bra.

His hand moves towards my shorts, and he stops after undoing the top button. “I’ve been thinking about this a lot,” he says in a quiet voice.

“Me too.”

He shakes his head. “Not as much as me.” His eyes move from my waist to my eyes. “I fantasize so much during the day that I dream about it at night.”

“Really?”

“Yes.”

I smile. “That’s sweet.”

“Me being a hornball is sweet?”

“As long as you’re thinking of me...yes.”

He takes a breath and lets it out, the warm air fanning over my exposed skin. “It’s always been you,” he says. And then he’s moving, kissing, touching me everywhere.

Our hands trail over each other like we’re memorizing each other’s form.

Somehow the rest of our clothes disappear and I have no recollection of how they were removed or where they went. The only sound in the room is our ragged breathing.

I escape from the haze of lust long enough to grab a condom from my nightstand. I bought some weeks ago with this exact moment in mind, except I have no idea what to do with it. I hand it to him and it’s awkward for the brief moment it takes him to open it and put it on as his body hovers over mine. His hands are shaking slightly.

“Are you okay?” I ask him, grabbing one of his trembling hands in mine.

“I’m just...really nervous.” His eyes search mine and he gives me a half-smile. “I want this to be perfect.”

"Hey, come here." I pull him down so we're lying side by side facing each other. This time I'm the one that slows us down. I cuddle into him, sliding a hand up and down his back. "Nothing is ever perfect," I tell him. "Perfection is boring. I prefer flawed and interesting. Besides, didn't you say it's our imperfections that make us perfect for each other?"

"I did say that," he remembers. "I'm pretty smart."

"And modest." I laugh.

He kisses my laugh away and we got lost in each other.

His hand trails down my leg, pulling it up and over his hip.

With a gentle thrust of his hips, he slides himself against me, making me shudder and gasp.

He watches my face as he pushes into me carefully, but only an inch or so, before he pulls out and rubs against me again. He continues this pattern with near-agonizing slowness, driving me to madness bit by bit.

He lowers his head to my breast and I come completely undone, shuddering and shaking and that's when he slides himself completely into me.

"Oh, wow," I whisper when I can speak.

He rolls onto his back, pulling me on top of him, still wrapped around each other.

He kisses my neck. "Is this okay?"

I sit up, looking down at him and adjusting my position until I feel comfortable.

He groans at my movements, making me smile.

"This is okay," I say.

His fingers grip my hips and he apparently can't take it anymore and thrusts up into me, making me gasp.

It takes a few minutes to get a rhythm down, but before long, we're moving together. Intense sensation and lust slowly build back into my body. Again.

My hands are on his chest, and I'm watching him react to our movements, which is turning me on even more.

He pulls my face down to his and presses his lips against mine. "I love you," he murmurs and then his body shudders underneath me. Watching him lose control tips me over the edge, and I follow him into bliss.

I collapse against his chest, my head resting in the nook between his shoulder and neck, body completely spent.

"Wow," he says while we're catching our breath.

"Yep."

"That was…" he trails off.

"Incredible," I finish.

His arms tighten around me. "I was going to say perfect."

"That was so not perfect," I scoff.

"It wasn't?"

"Not even close." I slide a finger down his chest. "We have to practice more." My hand moves even farther south.

"Oh, right," he says, beginning to get the idea.

"A lot more."

"I have no problems with this. I think we should start practicing right away. In the shower."

He sits up drawing me closer to him and then somehow getting us both off of the bed, while hiking me up in his arms.

I squeal and wrap my arms around his neck.

In his haste to get me into the shower, he runs my legs into the wall, making me laugh and smack him on the back of the head.

"Sorry about that. I'm a little eager to get started on this whole practicing thing."

Once in the bathroom, he sets me carefully on my feet and hugs me into his chest.

I look up into his face, those piercing blue eyes meeting mine with affection and love. "I hope we're never perfect," I say.

The End.

FOR VICTIMS OF RAPE

Freya's situation is not uncommon. Over 60% of rapes go unreported and 97% of rapists never spend a day in jail (https://www.rainn.org/statistics).

If you or someone you know is a victim of sexual assault, I hope you will report, or encourage the victim to report. Even if you don't succeed, you may save a future victim.

Although Lucy may understand and articulate the "biological urges" of homo sapien males, as a species, we have evolved to the point where we can control our urges. No always means no, whether you are male or female, and whether you are with a friend, boyfriend, husband, someone you've slept with before, or someone you are fooling around with now. The choice to share your body is always yours.

For more information, you can contact RAINN (Rape, Abuse & Incest National Network) at www.rainn.org or their hotline at 1-800-656-HOPE.

ALSO BY MARY FRAME

Imperfect Series reading order:

Book One: Imperfect Chemistry

Book Two: Imperfectly Criminal

Book Three: Practically Imperfect

Book Four: Picture Imperfect

Book Five: Imperfect Strangers

Book Six: Imperfectly Delicious

Looking for more nerdy romance?

Check out this dorky spin-off duet!

The Dorky Duet (Plus a companion novel!)

Rirdorkulous

Geektastic

Nerdelicious

The Extraordinary Series

Anything But Extraordinary

A Life Less Extraordinary

Extraordinary World

Coming June 2021

Time of My Life

ABOUT THE AUTHOR

Go here to sign up for the newsletter! www.
authormaryframe.com

Mary Frame is a full-time mother and wife with a full-time job. She has no idea how she manages to write novels except that it involves copious amounts of wine. She doesn't enjoy writing about herself in third person, but she does enjoy reading, writing, dancing, and damaging the eardrums of her coworkers when she randomly decides to sing to them. She lives in Reno, Nevada, with her husband, two children, and a border collie named Stella.

She LOVES hearing from readers and will not only respond but likely begin stalking them while tossing out hearts and flowers and rainbows! If that doesn't creep you out, email her at:
maryframeauthor@gmail.com

www.ingramcontent.com/pod-product-compliance
Lightning Source LLC
Chambersburg PA
CBHW061603190726
48288CB00007B/2158

* 9 7 8 1 9 5 4 3 7 2 0 7 8 *